THRE
A
CROWD

Other teen novels by Sophie McKenzie

Girl, Missing
Sister, Missing
Missing Me

Blood Ties
Blood Ransom

Split Second
Every Second Counts

THE MEDUSA PROJECT
The Set-Up
The Hostage
The Rescue
Hunted
Hit Squad

LUKE AND EVE SERIES
Six Steps to a Girl
Three's a Crowd
The One and Only

THE FLYNN SERIES
Falling Fast
Burning Bright
Casting Shadows
Defy the Stars

For older readers
Close My Eyes

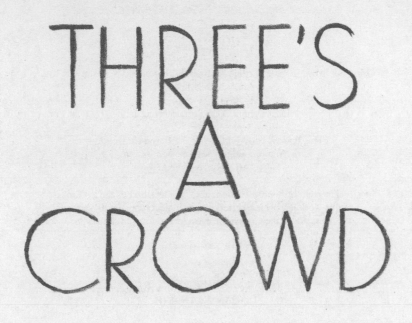

THREE'S A CROWD

Sophie McKenzie

Simon & Schuster

This edition published 2014

First published in Great Britain in 2008 by Simon and Schuster UK Ltd,
A CBS COMPANY

1 3 5 7 9 10 8 6 4

Simon & Schuster UK Ltd
1st Floor, 222 Gray's Inn Road
London WC1X 8HB

Simon & Schuster Australia, Sydney
Simon & Schuster India, New Delhi

A CIP catalogue record for this book
is available from the British Library.

PB ISBN: 978-1-47112-151-7
EBook ISBN: 978-0-85707-668-7

Printed and bound by CPI Group (UK) Ltd, Croydon, CR0 4YY

www.simonandschuster.co.uk
www.simonandschuster.com.au

For Katie, my w. k. f.

1
The plan

D'you want to know the worst thing about having a totally amazing girlfriend?

What's he on about, you're asking? How can there be a worst thing? How can there even be a downside? Especially with Eve. She's beautiful and sexy and fun and sweet.

And she likes me back.

Well, there *is* a downside.

It's all the other guys. The ones who wish they were with her instead of me.

I guess she gets about six boys a day hitting on her. And that's just an ordinary school day. If we go to a party or a club I can't leave her for a minute without them swarming round her like wasps.

Drives me mad.

Eve doesn't see it. She says they're just chatting. Being

friendly. But I know better. I know they don't care about her, like I do. I know they're just after one thing.

Most blokes are like that. Eve's previous boyfriend, Ben, was always trying to get her to do it with him. Yeah, Ben. He didn't like it when he found out I'd been seeing Eve.

But that's another story. I don't want to think about all that. I just want to think about Eve.

Eve and me.

It was the last week of the summer term. Eve and I were meeting after school in the Burger Bar. I like it there – they play good music and sell big portions at cheap prices.

I walked in a bit late, thanks to a heated discussion with my form teacher who says if I don't work harder I'm going to fail all my GCSEs next year. I saw Eve straight away. I always see her first in any room. That's not some weird, psychic connection by the way. It's her hair. Catches the light – all sleek and blonde.

She was sitting at one of the booths, her head bent over a plastic sheet menu. I could just make out someone else's arm on the other side of the table. A male arm. Whoever it was must have been sitting slouched down – I couldn't see his head and shoulders – but there was definitely someone there. Someone flirting with her. As usual.

I strode over, psyching myself up for the necessary

get-out-of-here-this-is-my-girlfriend look I was about to give.

Then I saw who it was. Ryan. I breathed a sigh of relief. Ryan's pretty much my best mate. He's going out with my older sister, Chloe. In fact that's how we got to know each other – when he was after Chlo and I was after Eve a few months ago.

"Hi, Luke." Ryan grinned up at me from his bench. "Eve and I were just talking about you."

"Oh, yeah?" I looked over at Eve. She was blushing, like Ryan had really embarrassed her. She had to have the sexiest, poutiest mouth in the history of the world.

I couldn't look at that mouth without wanting to kiss it.

I slid in beside her and leaned across. *Mmmn.*

I could hear Ryan making puking noises across the table. I didn't care. Eve pushed me gently away. Her eyes sparkled up at me.

"So what were you saying about me?" I asked.

"Um . . ." Eve looked away.

"Wait till Chloe gets here." Ryan nudged Eve across the table. "I've just called her. She'll be here any minute."

I frowned, wondering what was going on. Then Eve took my hand and I forgot everything else.

"You're here early," I said. This was a running joke between us. Eve is always, always late for everything.

"I *was* early, actually." Eve smiled.

"Eve has news," Ryan said, looking like he was trying not to laugh.

"What?" I said.

"Wait for Chloe," Ryan said again.

"Jesus, Ry. What's going on?"

"Come on, man. You know Chloe. She'll be furious if she's left out of it."

This was undoubtedly true, though not what I was asking. Chloe's not a bad sister. But she's an unbelievably moody human being. Ryan is the only person I know who has any kind of influence over her. And even he struggles sometimes.

It was at this point that Chloe turned up.

Ryan smiled. "Hey Pig Baby," he drawled in an exaggerated American accent.

"Hi, Skankface." Chloe grinned as she leaned over to kiss him.

Eve and I exchanged glances. Neither of us really get the way Ry and Chloe seem to enjoy being rude to each other. Sometimes they even have these terrible rows, where one or both of them completely lose it. You think they'll never speak again. But the next time you see them, they're back to being all loved-up.

Eve and I don't do that. We're totally into each other. Always.

"So what's this big deal news?" I said.

"It's my dad," Eve said. "He wants me to spend the whole of August at his new hotel in Mallorca."

I blinked at her, my stomach twisting into a knot. "The *whole* of August?"

"Yeah." Eve stared down at the table. I guessed she knew what I was thinking. A whole month apart. And I was so looking forwards to having loads of time together – the summer holidays about to start. And now we'd have . . . what . . . ten days before the end of July – then she'd have to go.

"Sounds cool," Chloe said. "Will your dad expect you to work at the hotel?"

Ryan broke into a fit of coughing.

"Yeah," Eve explained, still staring at the table. "I'll have to help out waiting tables and sorting things out by the pool and maybe even working in the crèche . . . but I guess it's still four weeks in Spain."

My heart was sliding down into my shoes. I was wrong. Four weeks away from me and she didn't even seem all that bothered.

Ryan recovered from his coughing fit.

"Does your dad run the place, then?" he said.

Eve nodded.

"Lots of staff?"

5

"Yeah – especially over the summer. He gets masses of English tourists, so. . ."

". . .he has to hire extra help," Chloe finished. She raised her eyebrows. "Mmmn. Imagine the buff Spanish pool boys."

I glared at her.

"Bet the girls are hot, too," Ryan added. "Go on, Eve."

Eve paused. "Actually my dad doesn't usually hire girls to work for him. He says they're too distracting for the male staff. And sometimes there are problems with the guests too. You know, middle-aged men trying it on. It's supposed to be a family place, so my dad tries to . . . to stop trouble starting by not hiring girls."

"Yet he's happy for *you* to go and work there?" I said, unable to control the angry shake in my voice. The idea of Eve being away for four weeks was bad enough. But knowing she'd be the only girl working in a hotel full of hot, pervy, Spanish guys and lecherous British tourists was unbearable."What about your mum? Won't she mind?"

But I already knew the answer to that. Eve's mum was nice, but basically pathetic. As far as I could gather from the stories Eve told me, she'd never stood up to Eve's dad once.

Eve wouldn't meet my eyes. I stared at her, Ryan and Chloe forgotten. Her lips twitched. Was she laughing at me?

I sprang to my feet, feeling utterly humiliated. "Great,"

I said sarcastically. "Hope you have a great time. Send me a postcard."

I turned to walk away. Eve grabbed my wrist.

"Luke," she said. "Stop. We're just messing around."

I turned back to her, pulling my arm free. "What?"

I caught sight of Ryan and Chloe – they were leaning against each other, shaking with silent laughter.

"I'm sorry," Eve said. "Listen, my dad loves girls." She blushed. "Too much, in fact. I certainly won't be the only one working there. But that's not the point."

"I don't get it." I looked from her to Ryan and Chloe.

"Sorry, man." Ryan grinned. "It was my idea. I called Chloe and told her before you arrived."

"But. . . ?"

"For goodness sake, Luke," Chloe sighed. "You are so easy. I mean, have you ever heard of a hotel that refuses to employ women?"

I shrugged, my face burning. It's not that I can't take a joke. I just don't like people taking the piss out of the way I feel about Eve.

Especially when Eve does it.

"That's not all," Eve reached out for my arm again. "Luke?" I looked at her. Her face was stricken. "I'm really sorry. Listen, it's brilliant. My dad said I could bring some friends if I wanted. That's the real news."

"What is?" I said.

"We're all invited. You, me, Ry and Chloe. Dad said it was okay. I mean, we'll have to do a bit of work while we're there, but we'll have loads of free time. The staff are mostly around our age and the hotel's got a virtually private beach. He says it's beautiful."

I sat down slowly, letting Eve wrap her arms round my neck.

"You mean we're *all* going, for all four weeks?" Relief was seeping through my feelings of anger and humiliation, washing them away.

Eve nodded, her eyes sleepily, sexily, inviting me to kiss her.

A smile crept round my mouth.

"If Mum says it's okay," Chloe said.

I drank in Eve's face again. "Oh, I'm sure that's not going to be a problem." I moved closer to her lips, suddenly feeling exhilarated. This was better than my wildest dreams. A whole month with Eve. In the same building. Not even having to go home at night. And August in Spain. It would be hot and. . .

"Luke." Chloe's voice barged into my mental picture of Eve sprawled across a beach in a bikini.

"What?" I said irritably.

"Put it away, dumb ass. The waitress is waiting to take your order."

2

Baby talk

Term ended. Mum had said she would think about the August holiday plan for a couple of days. I wasn't worried. I mean, what possible reason could she have for forbidding me and Chloe a free holiday?

And then I found the pregnancy test stick.

It was peeking out from under the other rubbish in the bathroom bin – a slim white cylinder with two holes on one side, each containing a thin blue line. I wasn't one hundred per cent sure what it was at first but Eve confirmed my suspicions when she turned up half an hour later. She took the cylinder carefully at the tips and examined it closely. She looked up at me with wide, fearful eyes.

"D'you think it's Chloe?"

"Who else?" I said.

I'd never thought before about how far Chloe and Ryan

had gone. I mean, they saw each other all the time but then so did Eve and I. And we weren't having sex. *Jesus.* I didn't want to think about it. Chloe's my *sister*.

"I'm going to ask her." Eve got up. "Is Ryan in there?"

I nodded. Eve walked across the landing and into Chloe's bedroom.

A minute later Chloe herself poked her head round the door.

"Luke," she said. "Come in here."

I dragged myself reluctantly towards her room. I couldn't imagine anything she might be about to say that I wanted to hear.

Chloe yanked me inside and shut the door. Eve and Ryan were sitting at opposite ends of the bed. They both looked up at me solemnly.

"It's not mine." Chloe shoved the little stick under my nose.

I stared at her. "But. . . ?"

"It's Mum. Gotta be."

My mouth dropped open. "No way," I said. "That's . . . that's . . . ew, that's disgusting."

"Well . . ." Eve raised her eyes. "It's certainly possible."

Matt.

My dad died seven months ago – January. That's where I first saw Eve, in fact – at his funeral. Matt was Dad's best friend.

Some friend.

He started trying to get it on with Mum almost immediately. Within two months they were going out together.

He's an idiot. A total prat.

"If they're having a baby he'll be unbearable," I groaned. "He sticks his nose in our business all the time anyway."

"Looks like he's stuck more than his nose in this time," Ryan smirked.

I gritted my teeth.

"Stop it, Ry," Chloe snapped. "We don't even know if it's true."

Ryan shrugged. "Well, go and ask your mum then," he said, flopping back on the bed.

Chloe and I left the others and traipsed downstairs.

We found Mum in the kitchen, taking a hunk of cheese out of the fridge. I prodded Chloe. No way was I doing the talking on this one.

"Mum?" Chloe cleared her throat.

Mum looked up from the fridge, a jar of pickle now in her hand.

"Sandwich?" she said.

"Food cravings?" I muttered under my breath.

"Is there anything you want to tell us?" Chloe said.

Mum stared at us, guiltily. Then her face cleared. "You mean the holiday?" she said. "Well, I've given it a lot of thought. I'm happy for you to go, but there's one condition."

I forgot about the pregnancy test stick. "What?"

Mum put the jar of pickle next to the cheese on the counter. "Homework," she said. "Every day."

"What?" Chloe snapped. "I've just sat my GCSEs – I'm not doing any freakin' homework."

"I didn't mean you." Mum narrowed her eyes. "It's you, Luke. Your report is terrible. All the teachers say you're going to fail your exams next year unless you make more effort."

I remembered my heated discussion with my form teacher from a few days ago. *You have the ability, Luke. Why won't you apply yourself?*

"I've got some Maths and English papers off the school. I want you to work on them over the holidays. Three hours every day." Mum said. She picked up a little knife and chopped a nugget of cheese off the chunk on the counter.

I couldn't believe it. "No way," I shouted. "That's *so* not fair."

"Fair or not, it's what's happening," Mum said. "If I don't get an email every day by two p.m. containing your work I will insist that Eve's father puts you on the next flight home."

I stared at her, open-mouthed.

"Mum," Chloe said. "Are you having a baby?"

Mum dropped her cheese knife onto the counter. I winced. Only Chloe would've come out with it like that.

"What?" Mum gaped at us. "How . . . how did you know?" she faltered.

Chloe glanced at me. I looked at the floor.

Chloe explained.

Mum stammered a bit as she told us the baby – due early next year – had come as a bit of a shock.

No shit, Mum. I was now fairly eager to leave the room. There's something totally gross about your mother having a baby, if you think about it too much. And then there was Dad. He'd only been dead seven months. I didn't want to think about that either. About how he would feel.

Chloe clearly had no such qualms. "What about Dad?" Her voice rose angrily. "I mean, are you even sure it's Matt's?"

Jesus. I started backing towards the door.

"Of course it is," Mum snapped. "And I don't appreciate you. . ."

I left the kitchen before Mum and Chloe started shouting at each other. I went back up to Chloe's room and pushed open the door, my head still reeling.

Eve was standing at the window, leaning against the sill. Ryan was lying back on Chloe's bed, hands under his head, staring up at the ceiling. It suddenly occurred to me that they'd been on their own together for at least ten minutes. They didn't look like they'd just torn apart from a lustful clinch, but still. . .

I squinted at Eve. She was staring at me, looking puzzled. *God*, she was hot. I glanced over at Ryan suspiciously. He wasn't obviously good-looking – wide mouth, long, sloping nose – but I knew most girls found him incredibly attractive. There was this laidback air about him and, if flirting was a sport, Ryan would be an Olympic gold medallist. Earlier this year he'd told me about these six steps which, he claimed, would get me any girl I wanted.

Get me Eve.

Of course it was all bullshit – Ry was just making it up to have an excuse to come round to our house and see Chloe. Still, most of what he said worked. And I had got Eve. Hadn't I?

"Well?" Eve said. "Is your mum really pregnant?"

"Yes," I said. "Now, d'you want the *really* bad news?"

It was the morning we were leaving for Spain. I was all packed, my bag weighed down by the ton of homework papers Mum insisted I was going to have to work my way through. Apparently she'd made sure there'd be a networked computer somewhere in the hotel for me to work on every morning. I still couldn't believe I was going to have to sit inside and study while everyone else had fun by the pool.

"Never mind," Eve had said. "We'll still have all afternoon and all evening."

This was true. In fact, the thought of it was what was keeping me going.

A soft rap on the door. "Luke?" Matt stuck his head into the room. "Can I have a word?"

I shrugged. My usual way of dealing with Matt was to pretend he didn't exist. I avoided speaking to him unless it was absolutely necessary, and we hadn't talked at all since I'd found out about the baby.

What was there to say?

The bottom line was that I hated the fact Mum was with Matt. None of the rest of it seemed real yet. Certainly not the idea of an actual baby. The one thing I had wanted to know was whether Mum getting pregnant meant Matt would move in with us. But Mum had said no – that they'd come to terms with the baby, blah, blah, blah, but that it was too soon after Dad for them to think about living together, blah, blah, blah, and that Matt still wanted his own space.

I'd said nothing, but inside I was deeply relieved. Matt

coming round was bad enough. Matt in the house full-time didn't bear thinking about.

"Your mum wanted me to talk to you before you left." Matt strolled across the room to the table in the corner. He picked up a pen and, turning to face me, rolled it in his hand.

"What about?"

"You know," he said. His face flushed a little.

I stared at him. *No. I don't.*

Matt tapped the pen against his hand.

"I don't have kids," he said, looking down at the floor.

"Yet," I added, pointedly.

Matt glanced up at me. "Er . . . right . . . yet. But I was your age once so I know what it's like."

What was he going on about?

"When you're on holiday, it's easy to get . . . er . . . carried away and well. . ." Matt's face went a deeper shade of red. "Your mum wants you to be careful."

It suddenly hit me.

Sex.

He was talking about me and Eve having sex.

Which we weren't. Unfortunately.

Which was none of his business.

"Why didn't Mum talk to me herself?" My chest tightened.

Man, the nerve of him. Lecturing me on "being careful".

"I guess she thought it would be easier for you to hear it from me." Matt tapped the pen faster against his hand. "Man to man."

"You mean she thought you'd be a good person to talk to me about . . . about . . . being *responsible*?" I raised my eyebrows.

Matt looked a little confused. "Well . . . er . . . yes, I . . ."
Unbelievable.

"Yeah. Well," I said sarcastically. "I can see why she thought you'd be a good person to explain how to avoid getting my girlfriend pregnant."

Matt shot a look at me. His face was almost purple. "Look, there's a big difference between you and Eve and what happened with us. We're adults, for a start, so—"

"Oh." I glared at him. "So getting someone pregnant by mistake's okay if you're old, is it?"

"Fine." Matt pushed himself away from my table. He clenched his fists, still holding onto my pen. "I'm sure your mum'll be pleased to hear about your attitude. Maybe she'll have a rethink about letting you go."

Bastard. How could you have ever been my dad's friend?

I itched to punch his stupid face.

Matt strode to the door.

No. No way was I going to let him stop me going on this holiday. "Wait."

Matt stood in the doorway. He turned round slowly and tapped my pen against his cheek. "Yes?"

"I'm sorry." I swallowed down my rage. "Tell Mum I'll be careful."

Unlike you were, you disgusting, pathetic excuse for a man.

A triumphant grin spread across Matt's face.

God. I hated him.

"Good." Matt chucked the pen at me and left.

I told Eve about the conversation with Matt while we waited for our flight at the airport. She looked totally amazing in this little strappy top she was wearing. Deeply sexy and yet somehow innocent at the same time.

"He was probably just trying to help," she said.

I frowned. "It's none of his business what we do," I said. "Is it?"

The truth was I was half hoping that Eve might be as annoyed by Matt as I had been. Maybe even annoyed enough to rethink her "not yet" position on sex.

This position was something that our relationship was based on – her previous boyfriend, Ben, had pushed her hard to go all the way. When Eve and I had started going out properly, she'd explained to me that sex just wasn't an option – yet. In fact, one of the main reasons she'd liked me was that I hadn't been pushy about it. That I'd agreed to wait for her to tell me when she felt differently.

I was still waiting.

Eve grinned. My heart sank. She didn't look the slightest bit annoyed. "Who cares what Matt says," she said. "We're going to have such a great time together." She leaned over and kissed me. Her tongue flickered lightly in my mouth, sending about a zillion megahertz of lust zapping straight to my groin. She pulled back and I opened my eyes. She was giving me this big, sexy smile. I watched the strap of her top slide off her smooth, creamy shoulder.

Oh, God. She was a drug. I was an addict. Waiting didn't come into it. It was irrelevant. I'd take however much she gave me. As often as she'd give it.

"D'you want a drink?" Eve pulled the strap of her top back up and peeled herself out of her seat.

I shook my head, turning round to watch as she sauntered over to the coffee bar. The young guy who was serving leaned on the counter to talk to her. Even though I couldn't see Eve's face, I knew she was smiling at him. Jealousy twisted in my stomach.

The coffee bar jerk stared at her bum the whole time she was walking back to me. I helped her gulp down her frappucino, then suggested we went to the gate for the flight.

"Why?" Eve looked irritated. "We've got loads of time."

Because I can't stand being here with that guy horning after you.

We caught sight of Ryan and Chloe snogging near the duty free shop. "Look at them," I muttered. "Don't they ever stop?"

Eve laughed her gorgeous, throaty laugh. "You can talk."

I stared at her. What did she mean? Was she saying I was too all over her? Was she saying she didn't want that? I looked around. Men everywhere were lusting after her. Some out of the corner of their eye. Some quite openly. When we first started seeing each other I remember liking the fact that she was so desirable. Now it just made me feel under pressure.

Under pressure to be better than the rest of them. The other guys.

Eve and Chloe went off to buy some magazines. I slumped into one of the airport lounge seats and listened to some music. After a few tracks I switched off my iPod and opened my eyes.

No sign of Eve.

"They're buying perfume now," Ryan said, stretching

out his legs in the seat opposite. "To attract the buff Spanish pool boys."

I stared at him, wondering how he could possibly be thinking that and looking so relaxed.

"Don't you mind?" I said.

"What? That Chloe fancies the idea of other guys?" Ryan grinned. "Be weird if she didn't, wouldn't it? We do. Other girls, I mean."

I shook my head. "That's different."

"Why?" Ryan laughed at me.

I shrugged. It was too hard to explain. Of course *I* noticed and fancied other girls. It was like a knee-jerk reaction that had nothing to do with how I felt about Eve. But for *her* it was different. If she wanted someone else, she'd get them – no question. And if she got them . . . I chewed on my lip. I'd go mad if I let myself even think about it.

Ryan leaned forwards, his fringe flopping over his eyes. "You need to calm down, man," he said. "Seriously. The worst thing you could do is get all clingy with her. Girls hate that."

He sat back. I jammed my earphones right into my ears and sank deeper into my seat.

3

Meeting Jonno

Towards the end of the two-and-a-half hour flight, Eve started fidgeting in her seat. Then she disappeared into the aeroplane toilet for so long I started to get worried she'd fainted or something.

At last she re-emerged. She'd changed out of the sexy, strappy top into a pink dress, a big T-shirty sort of thing with a teddy bear on the front.

"Why've you put that on?" I said.

"My dad got it for me." She sat back down next to me. Her forehead creased with an anxious frown. "Does it look okay?"

I stared at her. Eve was one of the least vain people I'd ever met. I couldn't remember the last time she'd talked about what she was wearing or asked me how she looked.

I took in the pink dress. It was a bit shapeless though at

least, I reflected, that might stop other blokes staring at her. More than that, though, it made her look about six years old. Eve smiled at me – a wobbly, uncertain smile.

"Luke?"

"You look great," I said, not knowing what else to say.

Eve gave a distracted little nod, then sat back in her seat. A minute later I turned round. A tear was trickling down her face.

Had I done that?

"Eve?" I leaned sideways and touched her arm. "What's the matter?"

She looked at me, her lips trembling. "It's just the thought of seeing my dad. I haven't – not since before I met you. It's always like that when he's setting up a new business and. . ." Another tear trickled down her face. ". . .I miss him and I always worry before I see him. D'you understand?"

I nodded, though I had no idea what she might be worrying about. This was something Ryan had taught me. Always look as if you're listening – even if you don't understand what they're talking about.

It seemed to work.

Eve snuggled up next to me. We kissed slurpily. But not for long. Unlike Chloe, who – I suspect – actually enjoys being watched mid-snog, Eve gets very self-conscious if we're anywhere remotely public. It's always, "not here", "not now".

Soon she pulled away from me. "Crap," she said. "I'll have to check my make-up. Daddy hates it if he thinks I'm wearing too much."

She disappeared into the toilets again. I sat back, feeling uneasy. I hadn't given Eve's dad a single thought so far. Now I wondered what he was going to be like.

At last we arrived in Mallorca. Palma Airport was nothing special on the inside. We might as well have been in London apart from the signs in Spanish everywhere.

Eve and I picked up our luggage off the conveyor belt and trundled behind Ryan and Chloe through customs. The air conditioning in the airport was set to icy. I noticed Eve shiver.

"It'll be warmer outside," I said, putting my arm round her shoulders. I'd grown a good couple of centimetres over the past few months and was now almost a head taller than she was. Her shoulder was at the perfect level for my arm. And, normally, Eve was perfectly happy for me to put my arm round her. Not today, though. She wriggled. Then she shrugged my arm off. Then she darted ahead of me, past Ryan and Chloe, towards the exit gate.

I frowned and sped up slightly. Not in a clingy, needy way. Just so as not to lose sight of her.

She rushed through the exit, her hair flying behind her.

I passed Chloe and Ryan.

"Why is Eve wearing a child's nightie?" I heard Ryan asking.

I gritted my teeth and headed into the arrivals area after Eve. It was packed. Crowds of people were jammed up against the barrier gates, peering in, looking out for their own particular new arrival.

I felt a twinge of jealousy as Eve darted about. Half the people behind the gates were staring at her.

Then Eve gave a squeal. She rushed towards the end of the barriers, where fewer people were standing.

A tall, well-built man stepped out from the crowd. He had slicked-back hair – as dark as Eve's was fair – and a tanned, slightly wasted face. It was easy to see that he must have once been very good-looking.

He grinned and threw his arms open wide. Eve flung herself at him, wrapping herself tightly round his neck. "Daddy," she shrieked.

Ryan and Chloe carried on sauntering towards them. I stopped, gripped by my most disturbing feelings of jealousy so far.

For goodness sake. He's her father.

I repeated this to myself several times. But it didn't lighten the heavy, sick feeling that was ploughing up my stomach as I watched Eve hugging him. I strolled up behind Chloe and Ryan.

Eve's eyes were shining. "This is Chloe," she said.

Her dad held out a large, be-ringed hand towards Chloe. "Beautiful," he murmured, rolling the word out slowly. "What a beautiful friend you have, Babycakes."

Chloe blushed. I glanced at Ryan. He was grinning.

That's Ryan all over. He appreciates good flirting. Whoever it's aimed at. Personally I was starting to think Eve's dad was a bit of a sleazeball cliché. His right hand was loaded down with gold rings and his shirt was open, revealing a bronzed chest.

"I'm John Ripley," Eve's dad said, pumping Chloe's hand and gazing at her with hooded eyes. "My friends call me Jonno."

He turned back to Eve. "You look lovely, Babycakes. More like your mother each time I see you." He raised his eyebrows. "How is her ladyship?"

"Fine," Eve lowered her eyes and picked at the teddy bear on her dress. "She says 'hi'."

I knew this was a lie. Eve's mother never talked about her father. Eve had told me many times. *He was the love of her life, then he ran off with a cocktail waitress when I was five. He gives her money and stuff, but she still feels really hurt – to be honest, I think she's scared of him.*

26

I stood awkwardly, wondering when Jonno (and what a freakin' stupid name *that* was) was going to notice me and Ryan.

He kissed the side of Eve's head and whispered something in her ear. At last he turned back to Chloe.

"So tell me, Chloe, which of these young men is your brother and which is your boyfriend?"

I frowned as Chloe introduced Ryan. There was something wrong. Why was Eve's dad not asking where *her* boyfriend was?

"And this is Luke."

I felt the full force of Jonno's steely grey-green eyes on my face. He looked stern – almost fierce. He shoved out his hand. Quick pump.

"Pleased to meet you," he said. Then he dropped my hand and turned back to Eve.

"Let's go, Babycakes." He put his arm round her shoulders. Right where mine had been just minutes before. "The car's outside."

I picked up my bag and Eve's and struggled after them.

Outside the heat hit me like a flamethrower. It was so steamily hot it was almost hard to breathe.

"Don't worry," Jonno said with a wave of his hand. "It'll be cooler when we get to the hotel. Less humid. Only idiot Brits come out at this time of day, anyway."

27

By the time we'd reached the car park and found Jonno's bright red Jeep Grand Cherokee, I was drenched in sweat. Somehow both Jonno and Eve had managed to remain relatively fresh-looking, though I was pleased to see Ryan pulling his damp T-shirt away from his chest.

"Man, it's hot," he said.

"Mmmn." I watched Jonno opening the passenger doors on one side of the car and ushering Eve and Chloe along the cool, leather seats.

"Which means just one thing . . ." Ryan nudged me in the ribs.

"What?" I said. Jonno had walked round the Jeep now and was getting into the driver's seat. I suspected he would quite happily have driven off and left me and Ryan behind.

"Girls in very, very skimpy clothes," Ryan hissed.

I nodded, distractedly. Eve hadn't even looked at me since we'd left the airport. It was like I didn't exist. I was suddenly transported back to the days when I used to watch her wandering around school, wondering whether I would ever have the courage to speak to her.

I sat, hunched, in a corner of the back seat as we pulled out of Palma Airport and through snarling queues of honking traffic. Jonno had put the AC on at full blast and I was soon shivering.

Jonno chatted away to the girls, one large hand spread

over the steering wheel, the other tapping on the side of the car door. Ryan, who was sitting immediately behind him, leaned forwards and joined in.

He asked loads of questions about the resort – where it was, how big it was – that sort of thing. Ryan's brilliant at talking to people. You could see Jonno warming to him, starting to volunteer all sorts of information.

"We're based just up the coast from Cala del Toro. South-east of the island. Nearest big town's Felanitx. Most of the British operations are in the north, round Pollença, but we've got a great spot. Not full, but for a first season we're not doing so bad. Not far off our rack rates on the suites anyway."

I watched the four of them, chattering and laughing as we left the traffic behind and sped along an open road. The sun was low in a clear blue sky and the landscape open – dry, rocky, straw-coloured ground stretching away towards green fields with olive trees and little stone cottages in the distance. We rounded a bend onto the coast road and saw the sea – dark blue in the distance, pale green near the bay below.

"Oh, it's beautiful," Eve gasped, leaning forwards.

She beamed up at her dad, then turned round and grinned at me.

I forced a smile onto my mouth.

You remembered I'm here, then?

Eve looked puzzled, but she didn't say anything. Just turned back and started chatting to her dad again.

The holiday was not, I felt, getting off to a good start.

4

Bonita rules

The light was starting to fade by the time Jonno slowed the car to pull through Cala del Toro. It was very quiet – road after road of old, tall terraced buildings with flower boxes at the windows. The main street was slightly busier, full of little shops with faded awnings.

We swung round a big stone plaza with a huge tree in the middle. Dotted around the edges were a series of tables and chairs, each obviously belonging to one of the cafes in the roads opposite the square.

They were mostly empty.

"Nothing much gets going till at least nine or ten here," Jonno said. "Later on the plaza'll be really happening."

Really happening? For goodness sake.

I glanced at Ryan, hoping to exchange a grimace, but he was staring out of the window.

A mile or so along the empty road out of Cala del Toro and we reached a high stone wall. Jonno slowed the Jeep.

"We're here. La Villa Bonita," he announced. "*Bonita* means pretty," he added, turning to Eve. "I named it after you."

"Da-ad," Eve murmured. But I could tell she was pleased. I scowled. What an idiot.

Jonno pulled the Jeep through an arch in the stone wall. A sprawling white building stood at the end of a long, dusty drive. Part of it was on two floors, the rest was flat-roofed and fronted with brightly coloured flowers.

I had to admit the effect was . . . well . . . pretty.

As Jonno stopped the car outside a long wooden porch, two guys in blue jackets appeared from nowhere, rushing to open both front doors. A whoosh of warm air entered the freezing car interior.

"*Hola, Señor Ripley,*" one of them said in a thick Spanish accent. "Good trip?"

"Yeah, cheers, Marco." Jonno jumped out and clapped the nearer of the two guys on the back. He was young. Probably no older than me or Ry. And quite short, with a slightly blobby nose. He grinned past Jonno to us in the back.

I scrambled out of the car, enjoying the feel of the warm air against my skin. It was still hot, but not humid any more, with a light breeze. In the distance I could hear the tumble and splash of the sea. Crickets rasped all around us. It was perfect, except . . . I looked at Eve. I was *sure* she was avoiding me now.

"Marco, take Ryan and Lance to their room will you?" Jonno said.

I glared at him. *Lance?*

Ryan sniggered, but Jonno didn't appear to notice.

"I'll show the girls to their rooms myself," he said. "Everyone meet in the lobby. Half an hour."

He stuck a fat cigar in his mouth, then flung his arms round Eve and Chloe and herded them towards the front entrance. I took a step after them, but Marco laid his hand on my arm.

"No that way, please," he said. "You follow me?"

Ryan and I were sharing a room round the side of the hotel. It was at the end of a long row – large and square, with a tile floor and two single beds.

Marco pointed to the TV in the far corner. "No Sky," he grinned. "Only Spanish TV."

"No worries, man," Ryan said. "We're not here to watch TV, 'cept maybe a bit of football."

Marco laughed. "You like Real Madrid? Everyone from England like Real?"

"Nah, I'm more of a Barca fan." And Ryan was off, chatting away like he'd known Marco for years. It turned out Marco lived nearby and was working at La Villa Bonita over the school holidays. I stood by the window tuning in and out of their conversation and staring at a patch of concrete outside. A low brick wall ran halfway across it, then just stopped, as if someone had started building and then given up.

I wondered where Eve was.

"My girlfriend has many friends," Marco was saying. "They like the English boys. Is same with us, liking the English girls."

I stomped off to take a shower.

When I came out Marco had gone and Ryan was lying on one of the beds, grinning. "That guy was cool," he said. "And there's loads of people our age here as well." He sat up. "This sharing a room thing isn't going to make any difference either."

I stared at him. "It freakin' is," I said. "You're not bringing Chloe back here."

Ryan laughed. "It stays hot outside until gone midnight, man. And the hotel's got its own private beach. Think about it."

The lobby was a short walk away, back inside the main part of the hotel. Jonno was chatting to the reception staff as we wandered through a sea of squashy-looking sofas and chairs. The place was fairly busy – like Eve had said, full of families with young kids.

Jonno saw us coming and strode over, a cigar still clamped to his lips. "Ryan. Lance." He slapped us both on the back. "Room okay?"

"Great, sir," Ryan said.

Sir?

I stared at Ryan. Where had that come from?

"What about you, Lance, got everything you need?" Jonno grinned at me.

"It's Luke," I said. "My name. Not Lance. Luke."

Jonno nodded vaguely. He looked up. "Here they are, the original Bonitas."

I followed his gaze. Eve and Chloe were wandering through the door at the other end of the lobby. They drifted slowly towards us, attracting admiring glances from the entire room. They were both wearing short dresses and their hair looked different, though I couldn't exactly work out how. Eve's dress was all clingy and swishy, floating out over the tops of her long, slim legs.

She looked totally amazing.

I jerked forwards as Jonno slapped me on the back again. He put his arm round me and gripped my far shoulder. I could see he had Ryan on the other side in exactly the same position.

"Now boys." He forced us into this standing huddle, leaning his head down so it was nearer ours. "You're Eve's friends and I want you to have a good time while you're here. We'll talk about the few jobs I want you to do tomorrow. But I want you to feel free to have fun here. *Mi casa es tu casa* and all that. Understand?"

I nodded, wishing he would let go of my shoulder.

Jonno dug his fingers in harder. "But there are two rules. And they're non-negotiable. Break them and you leave. Immediately." He paused. "The first: do nothing – I repeat *nothing* – that will embarrass my guests. Get as pissed as you like, but in your own time and not in any of the public areas. Shag whoever you like on the staff, but no holiday romances with the clients. Okay?"

I nodded. I could see Ryan doing the same on Jonno's other side. I tried to move away. Jonno's hands were like clamps. His grip tightened even further. Then he let go of Ryan and looked straight at me.

"Second rule. Whatever you were hoping would happen with my daughter while you were out here – forget it. Do not touch her. Do not so much as lay a single finger on her. I will know if you do."

What? I stared at him, my heart pounding. Surely he must know Eve and I were going out together? *Surely* she must've told him?

"Go anywhere near her and you'll be out of here as fast as I can kick you. Via a hospital, probably. Geddit?"

36

Jonno glanced at Ryan, who nodded fervently at him. Then he turned to me. "Lance?" he said.

I looked down at the floor. "I hear what you're saying," I stammered. "Sir."

"Good." Jonno at last released us with a final slap on the back. He strode forwards to greet Eve and Chloe. I caught Ryan's eye.

"The man's a lunatic," Ryan said, a note of admiration in his voice. "Glad I'm not you, mate."

I rubbed my bruised shoulder.

Jonno kissed Eve and Chloe on both cheeks, then strode over to the reception desk. The girls drifted up to us. Ryan started in on how fabulous Chloe was looking. Eve looked up at me expectantly. I blinked, still trying to make sense of what Jonno had said. There was only one explanation.

"You didn't tell him."

Eve frowned. "Who? What?"

"You didn't tell your dad I was your boyfriend," I said, my anger mounting. "Why? Are you ashamed of me or something?"

Eve looked round nervously.

"We're going for a walk," Ryan said. He and Chloe slipped away.

Eve and I sat down in the squishy chairs.

"Well?"

Eve flushed. "He gets so weird about me dating guys. I thought he might not let you come if I told him. I was going to say something once we arrived. I haven't had a chance yet."

I told her what Jonno had said to me and Ryan. "And the way he said he'd know if anyone touched you made it sound like he had hidden cameras everywhere – or spies watching out for you."

Her face fell. Then she looked up at me. "It doesn't need to matter that much, does it?"

"What?" I gaped at her.

"I mean we can still hang out together."

I couldn't believe my ears. "But I won't be able to kiss you, or . . . or anything."

"So?" Eve's eyes narrowed. "Is that all you care about?"

"Of course not, but . . . but. . ."

She folded her arms. "But what?"

"You're my girlfriend."

Eve shrugged and looked away. "I still am. It's just . . . we have to be careful. That's all."

I sat back in my chair, defeated. I was sure Ryan would have come up with something that would have rescued the situation, but whatever that something was, it was way beyond me.

5

La hija del jefe

Eve stayed in a mood with me until Jonno appeared to usher us all into the dining room for our evening meal. He explained that the hotel had two sittings – one for all the young families at six, and another, at eight, which was a bit more grown-up.

We went in early for the second sitting, in time to see several hotel staff scurrying about picking up what looked like the remains of a food fight off the floor.

Eve saw me looking around and sidled up.

"Never eat at six," she whispered. "The English kids are disgusting." She ran her fingers down the inside of my arm. "Though maybe you should – get you in practice for having a baby brother or sister."

The touch of her hand was so distracting I walked straight into the back of a chair coated with tomato ketchup. I looked down. A dark red line was smeared messily across my crisp white shirt. *Crap*.

"I'll show you where the bathrooms are," Eve said quickly.

I glanced at Jonno, but he was deep in a football conversation with Ryan. We slipped out, but instead of heading to the door marked *Servicios/Toilets*, Eve doubled back round the side of the main lobby and led me up the main staircase to the first floor.

"Where are we going?" I said.

"My room," she smiled. "You can use the bathroom there."

She slid her card key through a door stamped with the words *Privado/Private*. The corridor beyond immediately felt different to the rest of the hotel. Messier and homier, with magazines and mugs of old coffee on the tables and photos of Eve and Jonno lining the walls.

I caught sight of one of Eve, aged about seven, wearing a long, white dress with some sort of tiara on her head. It was similar to a picture in her mum's house, except that in this one she was holding Jonno's hand.

"From when I made my first Holy Communion." Eve made a face. "Daddy's idea. God knows why. He's about the most lapsed Catholic you could meet."

I looked at the photo again. Under the little tiara, Eve's blonde bob hung straight and smooth, not a wisp of hair out of place. The blue ribbon on the front of her dress was tied in a perfectly-formed bow. "You look like a doll," I said.

"Yeah, I know. Come on." Eve walked away, pointing to the doors on the left as she passed them. "Mini-kitchen. Dad's room. Guest room. Big bathroom. Living room." She stopped at the two doors right at the end. "Chloe," she pointed to the one on the left. "And me."

"Mmmn," I said. "So you're as far away from the rest of the hotel as he can get you."

"I know." Eve grimaced. "At least there aren't any security cameras in here."

She opened the door and I followed her into a huge bedroom. A big double bed with floaty pale pink material hanging around it stood in the middle of the far wall. Huge white closets, roses on the curtains, an ornate dressing table with a big china doll on top. It was nothing like Eve's bedroom at home.

I screwed up my face. "Bit little girly isn't it?"

Eve sighed. "This is who Dad thinks I am. His only child – a little girl dreaming of dolls and pink cushions." She started unbuttoning my shirt. "He's got no idea."

I looked down at her long slim fingers. The nails scraped gently across my stomach as she slid her fingers round the buttons.

How horny was that?

I put my arms around her. "Won't he get suspicious if we don't go straight back?"

Eve looked up at me. She grinned. "I was just going to rinse the ketchup off your shirt," she said.

"Oh. Oh yeah." I tugged off my shirt and followed her through a door in the corner of her room into the bathroom. It was all swirly white furniture and mirrors. The counter was littered with pots and lotions and tubes.

Eve held the ketchup stain under running water. I came up behind her. We looked at each other's reflection in the mirror.

"I'm sorry about earlier." Eve's face flushed. "It's just so weird being here with you *and* my dad." She wrung out the shirt, then smiled up at me.

I slid my hands round to the front of her dress.

"You look amazing." I bent down and kissed her neck.

Eve laughed, wriggling away from me. "Listen." She turned round. "We'll have to be careful in the hotel, but outside we should be all right. We'll still have lots of time together." She looked up, into my eyes. "Starting later tonight. Okay?"

"Good." I tried to kiss her again.

"Later," she said firmly.

I put my damp shirt back on and we went downstairs. Back in the dining room all the mess had been cleared away and the tables were transformed with white cloths and sparkling silver candles. The room was starting to fill up with hotel guests – mostly couples and families with older kids. Jonno shot me a fierce look as we came back to the table. Determined not to flinch, I stared right back at him.

"I was just showing Luke where the bathrooms are." Eve pointed to the faded ketchup stain on my shirt.

"And *I* was just telling Chloe and Ryan that the night-club's closed tonight. Still." Jonno's face softened as he looked at Eve. "You'll enjoy the Open Mike Night tomorrow. And Lola'll be back then too."

I glanced at Eve and mouthed "Lola?"

"Dad's latest girlfriend," she said in a disapproving voice.

Jonno grinned. "You're gonna love her, Babycakes. But tonight, while I've got you to myself, let's catch up. Leave the others to explore."

My heart sank. I stared at Eve, willing her to defy him, to say she wanted to explore too. But she was looking down at the tablecloth. *Crap.* She was already nodding her head.

"Sure Daddy," she said in this babyish voice. "I'd love to."

After the meal, Jonno and Eve disappeared upstairs. Chloe, Ryan and I sat in silence for a couple of minutes, then Chloe leaned over and kissed Ryan.

43

"Shall we go outside?"

Ryan grinned. "Fancy another 'walk' then, Pig Baby?"

Chloe grinned back. "You should be so lucky, Skankface."

I saw Ryan glance sideways at me.

Chloe rolled her eyes. "Okay."

Ryan slapped me on the back. "Come on, Babycakes," he boomed in a not bad impression of Jonno's voice. "Marco told me where the staff hang out."

I followed them out through the main lobby and onto the terrace outside. The two wings of the hotel stretched out on either side, with a large lit-up swimming pool in-between.

Fairy lights hung from the trees that led down to the pool. Most of the sunbeds were stacked in a corner, but one was out. A couple lay on top of it, quite still in each other's arms. They weren't talking, just looking up at the sky.

I sighed. Eve was a total sucker for romantic places like this. Still, we had plenty of time, I consoled myself. There would be other nights.

I followed Ryan and Chloe round the pool and down through a little wooded area to the beach. The tide was out, the dark sea hissing in the distance.

We sauntered along the sand a few hundred yards until we came to another wooded area on the left. Through the trees I caught a glimpse of a row of wooden cabins. The sound of dance music drifted towards us across the sand.

"Staff quarters," Ryan said. "The bigger building on the end's where they come after work. Marco said it's called . . . what was it, Chlo?"

"El Garito." Chloe said. "It literally means a place for gambling. But here it just means Party House."

Ryan stepped over and pushed open the door. Inside the music was deafening, the bass pumping through the floorboards like a frantic heartbeat. The room was dark – just a few lights round the sides – and packed with people. Some of them were standing around chatting – cigarettes and beer bottles in their hands. Others were snogging in corners. Most were writhing in waves to the music, arms curving down and round – hard, urgent, insistent.

We stood by the entrance and looked around. The air was heavy with heat. It smelled of sweat and smoke and beer.

"Wow," Chloe shouted. Ryan nodded.

Marco appeared, weaving his way towards us through the throng of dancing bodies. He was smiling, holding hands with a petite, dark-haired girl in a short skirt.

"*Hola*," he shouted. "This my girlfriend. Catalina."

Catalina smiled up at us. She had a tiny, oval face and huge brown eyes. As her gaze met mine, her eyes narrowed slightly in this really sexy way.

She leaned across and touched my arm. "You can calling me Cat," she shouted.

45

Marco indicated we should follow him to the far end of the room. As we walked, the music got quieter. My eyes fixed on Catalina's skirt, on the way it clung to the tops of her slim legs as she wiggled sexily after Marco. She had a massively hot body – all compact and curvy.

She turned round suddenly and looked at me. I swallowed, wondering if she'd noticed me staring.

We all sat down in a corner. Marco vanished to get us some beers.

Chloe waved her hand towards the people smoking behind us. "Doesn't Mr Ripley mind all the drink and stuff?" she said to Cat.

She had to repeat the question, miming, partly because of the noise that still raged around us, partly to help Cat understand what she meant. Cat's face broke into a smile.

"No," she said. "Señor Ripley is good boss. He only have one rule. No make problem for guests."

Ryan nodded. "Yeah, we heard. Plus hands off his daughter."

This had to be repeated to Cat several times as well. At last she grinned again. "*Si*. The boys are telling me this new rule."

Ryan caught my eye. "At least you don't have to worry about any other guys while we're here," he said.

Marco came back with a clutch of beer bottles in his

hands. He offered them round. We sat chatting for a while. Then Ryan and Chloe went off to dance and some of Marco's other friends came and sat down. They spoke less English than Marco or Cat, but smiled and nodded at me. I was onto my second beer, leaning back in my chair, soaking in all the smells and sounds, when I realised they were talking about Eve.

I couldn't follow their rapid Spanish, of course. But I was sure I could make out her name being repeated, like I'd heard Marco say it when we arrived. *"Eva, Eva"*, though it came out *"Ay-va"*.

I stared at them. I didn't know what any of their words meant. But from the looks on their faces and their hand gestures, I was pretty sure I understood what they were saying.

One of the boys, a thickset guy standing next to Marco, reminded me of Eve's ex-boyfriend, Ben. I shuddered, my mind temporarily dragged back to the night he'd beaten me up.

At the time Eve had been two-timing him with me, so he'd had a right to be angry. But he'd gone well over the top – attacking me with two friends, leaving me bleeding and semi-conscious on the ground. I still got jittery sometimes at night – when I was out late on my own.

I forced my mind back to the Spanish boys' conversation. "Eva. Eva."

They were definitely talking about her.

I looked over at the thickset guy. He had this horrible leering expression on his face.

"*Quisiera morrearla*," he growled suggestively.

The others all laughed.

"*Estás loco*." That was Marco. "*Eva es la hija del jefe*."

I turned to Cat. "What are they talking about? What does 'lyee-ha-del-effy' mean?"

Cat stretched out her slim arms in front of her. "*La hija del jefe*," she said. "The boss's daughter. Eva? They are saying she is – it is a bit rude – they are saying she is good to look at. Do things to. Except her father say 'no'. You know?"

I nodded, grimly.

"You like her?" Cat's hand brushed lightly across my leg. "You like *la hija del jefe*?"

I stared at her. Her eyes were laughing at me. They were a deep, dark brown, the colour of chocolate.

"She's my friend," I said, uncertainly.

Cat narrowed her eyes again. "Just the friend?"

I nodded, feeling only slightly guilty.

It wasn't like I was pretending I didn't have a girlfriend out of choice. Anyway, for all I knew, Jonno could be paying his staff to spy on us.

Better just to keep it quiet.

Soon after that, Marco dragged Catalina off to dance. I wandered around for a bit longer. The music was still playing loudly and more people kept arriving, presumably those who'd been on later shifts. I didn't recognise anyone any more. And there was no sign of Ryan or Chloe. I guessed they were outside, somewhere on the beach.

I trudged back to the room, alone.

6

Jobs for everyone

I woke up the next morning feeling far better than I had when I'd got back to the room the night before. The sun was shining. Apart from Jonno himself, I liked everything about La Villa Bonita. And, on top of all that, I was going to see Eve: this morning; then, again, this afternoon – once I'd got my homework for Mum out of the way; and – with a bit of luck – this evening as well.

I glanced across at Ryan's bed. He was lying half in and half out of it, one arm hanging down to the floor, his fringe flopping over his face.

I checked the time. Ten-forty-five a.m. We had fifteen minutes before Jonno had told us to be by the pool to hear about the jobs he expected us to do. Eve had said it would just be a few hours each day. Another chance to do stuff together, I hoped.

My skin smelled of other people's cigarettes from the Garito last night. *Ugh.* I darted into the shower and scrubbed myself clean. When I re-emerged, towelling dry my hair, Ryan was sitting up in bed, groaning.

"Oh, God." He clutched theatrically at his head. "I am sooo fried."

"What happened?" I said.

He groaned again. "Beaches are not all they're cracked up to be. Not when you're with a high-maintenance babe, anyway."

"What d'you mean?"

"They're hard and they're cold," he said. "Next time I'm taking blankets."

I grinned. "Chloe insist on going back to her room then?"

Ryan nodded. "I was trying to sneak back up there with her, but Jonno caught me. He was out by the pool boozing with some of the guests. The man's a freakin' machine. Never stops. Must've been three a.m. He came after us. Told me to get lost. Only not so politely."

I raised my eyebrows. "Nice that he feels responsible for Chloe, though," I said, more to wind Ryan up than because I thought it was true.

Ryan snorted. "He doesn't give a toss about Chloe. He just doesn't want anyone male within striking distance of you-know-who."

My good mood deflated a little at this reminder of Jonno's over-protective attitude to his daughter – and at Eve's willingness to go along with it.

"You better get ready," I snapped. "We've gotta be by the pool in five."

Ryan lurched unsteadily out of his bed, still clutching his head. "I need more sleep," he said. "I didn't get back here till five-thirty."

I frowned. "But you said. . .?"

"I went back to the Garito, didn't I?" Ryan staggered into the bathroom. "More beers. More dancing. If it goes on like this I'll be dead by Friday."

I heard him splashing water on his face. He reappeared in the doorway, a toothbrush in his hand, looking slightly less wrecked.

"You were a big hit, by the way," he said.

"How d'you mean?"

"Marco told me. He's a really nice guy, you know. He said all the girls who work here were talking about you. Calling you *El Rubio* or something."

"What's *El Rubio* mean?"

"The Blonde."

I stared at myself in the mirror. My hair was brown. Light brown. Maybe with a few blondish streaks in the fringe, but. . .

Ryan appeared behind me in the mirror. "I know," he said. "I told Marco you aren't really blonde, but maybe out here they're not so fussy. Well, clearly they're not so fussy if they think you're hot . . . *Ow*."

He ducked as I swung my damp towel at him.

A massive bang on the door made us both jump.

"Ry. Luke." It was Chloe. "Get your arses out here. We're going to be late."

We caught Chloe up by the side of the hotel. It looked completely different in the bright sunlight. A little less smart. A lot less romantic. Kids were running about everywhere, weaving their way through the trees beyond the pool area down to a packed section of beach.

The pool area itself was bustling with people – adults lying out on the loungers and screaming kids in the water.

As we strolled up to the pool I noticed Marco pushing a large trolley laden with towels across the decking that led down to the pool from the hotel terrace. He grinned and waved.

I wondered vaguely where Catalina was. And then I saw Eve. She was standing with Jonno at the bar at the opposite end of the swimming pool. She was wearing a pair of tiny denim shorts and a bikini top. *Jesus*. I practically keeled over on the spot.

Ryan punched my arm. "I wouldn't let him see you looking at her like that, man," he said.

Gulping, I looked away.

Seconds later Jonno loomed up in front of us.

He pressed his hands down on my and Ryan's shoulders and leered at Chloe.

"Okay," he said. "Jobs. Jobs for everyone. I've decided that the girls should do five two-hour shifts a week on either crèche or pool duty and the boys the same but pool duty only – that means fetching soft drinks, towels, clearing up. Rest of the time you're all waiting tables, except Saturday – that's changeover day – when everyone pitches in to help out with anything needs doing. Right?"

We all nodded. Jonno held up a bunch of pink and blue T-shirts.

"You can wear your own shorts or skirts with one of these. That's the uniform, except when you're waiting tables, but you'll get kitted out for that later. Oh, and here's the schedule. Okay?"

Without waiting for a reply, he shoved the T-shirts at Ryan and a piece of paper at Chloe and strode off.

Ryan held out the T-shirts. There were two sorts. A tiny pink version with the words Bonita Babe written over the front in swirly lettering and a larger blue one with blockier type. It said Bonita Boy.

I frowned. Hadn't Jonno said *"bonita"* meant "pretty"?

"D'you realise what that means?" I said.

"Yeah." Ryan was staring disgustedly at the blue T-shirt. "It means Jonno wants everyone to think all his male staff are gay."

I looked over to the pool bar. Eve was still standing with her back to us, chatting to the barman. I had a flashback to the barman at the airport who had stared at her bum. I looked round the pool area. A lot of the men were throwing surreptitious glances in her direction.

I gritted my teeth.

"This isn't too bad, though." Chloe leaned against Ryan and pointed to the paper Jonno had given her. "It's really only a few hours a day – and look, we're together here and here, and we're waiting tables at the same time on Wednesdays, Thursdays and Sundays."

I glanced at the timetable. "What about me and Eve?" I said.

Chloe made a face. "He seems to be keeping you apart."

I snatched the paper out of her hand. It was true. I was free when Eve was in the crèche. She was free when I was on pool duty. And we were never waiting tables at the same time either.

"Arsehole," I muttered.

"Who?" said a familiar raspy voice behind me. I spun round. Eve was smiling up at me.

"Your dad." I explained about the timetable.

"I know," she said. "But we'll still have a few hours here and there and all the evenings."

I stared at her. Why wasn't she more upset?

We wandered up to the main lobby. As we reached the hotel we had to stand back and wait as a loud family with a never-ending stream of pasty-faced children barged through the doors in the opposite direction.

I glanced at Eve, wondering when we'd get a chance to be on our own.

"Oh my God." The urgency in Chloe's voice made me look up. She was watching a woman in tight, cropped jeans and very high heels tottering away from us, towards the pool loungers.

"What?" I stared at the woman. Her tiny bum wiggled as she reached into her handbag for a pair of sunglasses.

"Yeah, what?" Ryan said. "I mean it's very nice of you to point out attractive birds for us Chloe, but. . ."

"Wait till she turns round," Chloe said.

We all stared at the woman. She was now bending over a lounger, spreading out a towel. Then she straightened up and turned round.

My jaw dropped.

"They're enormous," Ryan breathed.

"Like beach balls," Eve whispered.

Chloe pursed her lips. "There's no way those are real," she said authoritatively.

The woman was causing something of a stir down by the pool. Nearly everyone was watching as she hooked her fingers into her tight, white T-shirt and peeled it over her massive chest and straining bikini top.

"God, she could take someone's eye out with those," Ryan gasped. "I need to sit down."

"It's because she's so slim everywhere else," Chloe said thoughtfully. "Makes the boobs look bigger. Though they're definitely fake."

"Oh, no," Eve whimpered.

Jonno was standing on the other side of the woman's lounger. He had put on a pair of sunglasses and was grinning. The woman laughed. She was clearly enjoying all the attention she was getting. Jonno reached over and stroked a strand of long, black hair off her cheek.

Eve hid her face in her hands. "How can he do this to me," she wailed. "It's so embarrassing."

"D'you think that's . . . whatsername?" Ryan said. "Your dad's *girlfriend*?"

Eve nodded. "Lola," she said, bitterly. "'S gotta be. She's even younger than his last one. And those . . . those. . ."

We all knew what she was referring to.

I put my hand on her shoulder. Her skin felt warm and soft. She wriggled away. "For goodness sake, Luke."

Jonno looked up at us. I whipped my arm down by my side. Did he have some kind of Eve-touching radar?

He started walking towards us. The smile on his face was gone.

"D'you think he saw me?" I said nervously.

Jonno pulled off his shades as he moved into the shadow of the hotel building.

"He's definitely looking at you, man." Ryan backed away.

It was true. Jonno's eyes were fixed on me.

"God, I put my hand on your shoulder for, like, two seconds," I hissed.

I could feel Eve shuffling nervously beside me. But my eyes were locked on Jonno's. I was trying to make out his expression. He looked so serious. Not angry, though. But then I remembered his number one rule. There was no way he would do anything in front of the guests.

Crap. Crap. Crap.

He strode up, running his large, ring-heavy hand through his hair. Now he was here, standing in front of us. Out of the corner of my eye I noticed that Ryan and Chloe had vanished.

"Forgot to show you where the computer is, Lance," Jonno said.

I gulped. Was this a trick? A way of getting me somewhere private so he could beat me up?

"Computer?"

Jonno frowned. "Yeah. For the daily homework your mum told me you'd got to do."

The homework. I'd forgotten all about it.

Jonno pointed me towards the door.

"Wait here, Eve," he said. "When I come back I want to introduce you to Lola."

As Jonno pulled open the door, Eve and I exchanged mutually pitying glances.

Then I followed Jonno inside the hotel.

7

Catalina

It took me three hours to get Mum's stupid homework done. I had to write an essay, a review of a fictional sporting event, then do twenty questions off a sample maths paper.

It was impossible to concentrate. Jonno had set me to work in an unairconditioned broom cupboard near his office. Well, maybe it wasn't an actual broom cupboard. But that's what it felt like. There was just room for the desk, the computer and me. Oh. And a small window which gave tantalising views of the far corner of the pool and the trees beyond.

The screaming of the kids in the pool was distracting enough, but every so often I'd also catch a glimpse of Eve, wandering about on the grass in her bikini.

I thought about ringing her mobile and asking her to

come and talk to me through the window, but decided against it. If I did that I wouldn't be finished until midnight.

After about an hour I was starving, but I didn't dare stop working. Mum had said she expected an email every day by two p.m. or she'd make Jonno send me home. And, having met Jonno now, I was sure he'd have no qualms about getting rid of me.

Sweating and grumbling under my breath I worked my way through both exercises, stopping only to email Mum to ask for an extension to the deadline.

At about quarter to two there was a knock at the door. Marco poked his head round. "*Hola.*" He grinned. "Eva give me this for you." He produced a large ham and cheese sandwich.

I fell on it, thanking him gratefully.

"She come herself, but she goes to the crèche now," Marco added.

Great. Just as I'm finishing up, Eve has to work.

I turned back to the computer and checked my emails. There was one from Mum, refusing my request for an extended deadline and saying:

"Matt, me and the bump all fine – thanks for asking."

Yeah, well Mum, I've got other things on my mind right now. Like doing your stupid homework and avoiding Eve's psychotic dad.

61

"PS: I had a scan yesterday. It's too early to tell, but I'm certain it's a boy. Thought you'd be pleased."

Pleased? Why would I be pleased? I don't care if it's a boy or a girl. They both make the same amount of noise, i.e. loud.

The shrill screams from the pool got worse as the afternoon went on. That, and the heat radiating into the room, only added to my worsening mood. I finally finished off the homework and emailed it off to Mum without replying to her message about the baby. It was two-fifteen p.m.

Outside the air was boilingly hot. Only a few hard-core sunbathers were still lying on loungers by the pool. I found Ryan in their midst, eyes shut, listening to my iPod.

I wrenched out the earphones.

"Hey." He sat up.

"I'm so pissed off." I kicked at his lounger.

"Yeah, well, don't take it out on the furniture." He grinned. "Jonno'll make you repaint it."

I sank down on the lounger next to his. "When do Eve and Chloe finish at the crèche?"

"Four o'clock." Ryan lay back and closed his eyes again. "But don't go getting excited. That's when we start waiting tables. Apparently the four-to-six shift's the easiest though. Mostly tea and cake and clearing tables. No proper meals or actual waiting or anything. Catalina's gonna swing by in an hour, pick us up, show us what to do."

"Oh?" I said.

Ryan opened one eye. "You fancy her, don't you?"

"No," I said.

Ryan laughed. "You are the world's worst liar, man."

I kicked at his lounger again. How annoyingly typical of Ryan to have sussed that I thought Cat was really hot.

"Well, don't you?" I said.

"Sure." Ryan sat back smugly. "But I'm with Chloe."

"And I'm with Eve," I said, feeling more irritated.

Ryan snorted. "Not so's anyone would notice, you aren't. And anyway," he crossed his arms, "Cat's with Marco."

"For goodness sake, Ry, I'm not going to do anything," I shouted, suddenly furious with him.

One of the hardcore sunbathers sat up and glared at me. Ryan shook his head, his eyes all wide and mocking.

"Don't embarrass the guests," he mouthed.

Another time I would have laughed. But right then I just felt too annoyed. I lay back on my lounger and sighed deeply. At this rate I was going to end up spending less time with Eve while we were on holiday than I did when we were at school.

*

63

Catalina showed up half an hour later in the waiting staff girl's uniform of black mini-skirt and tight, white blouse.

As she led us up to where we were picking up our own uniforms (black trousers and white shirts) Ryan murmured. "One thing you gotta say about Jonno – he likes his female staff in hot clothes."

"Mmmn," I grunted, trying not to stare too obviously at Catalina's slim, brown legs.

Clearing the tea tables wasn't too bad. Better than being in the kitchen, which felt like a sauna. Not many people showed up, and Ryan, Cat and I were able to spend most of our two-hour shift chatting.

Cat was even friendlier than she had been last night. She had this habit of touching me, all the time. A little stroke of the arm or a ruffle of the hair or a pat on the back.

"It's like she can't keep her hands off you," Ryan hissed as we passed each other on the way to the kitchen. I deposited my armful of dirty plates, then crossed the room to where he was refilling a china bowl from a large, encrusted jar of strawberry jam.

"She's like that with everyone," I said.

"Nah, mate." Ryan grinned at me. "For example, take me. She likes me, sure. But with you it's different. She's totally hot for you." He shook his head. "Poor Marco."

I shrugged. But inside, I had to admit I was pleased. Well,

why shouldn't I be? Cat was gorgeous. And it didn't mean anything was going to happen – after all, I *was* with Eve, whatever stupid games we had to play to hide it from her dad.

Cat left at the end of the shift, having extracted promises from both of us to turn up at the Garito that night.

"It start later Tuesdays," she said, looking up at me seductively. "Open Mike Night is popular. So many staff no free until late."

Ryan and I went back to our room to change. On the way we met Chloe who told us that Eve was having tea out with her dad and Lola.

I swore. "When am I supposed to see her?"

Chloe gave me a pitying look. "She said she'd catch us in the nightclub at nine. Her dad's offered to buy us some beers at the Open Mike. What are you going to sing?"

"I'm not," I said shortly. Personally, I thought the idea of an evening where people could get up and sing whatever they wanted sounded stupid.

Chloe put her arms round Ryan and gazed up at him adoringly. "What about you, Skankface?"

Ryan grinned. "I am surprising you," he said, "with my awesome talents." He pulled her into a snog as we reached the trees.

I stomped on ahead, muttering darkly to myself.

*

The nightclub was buzzing when we turned up at nine. The whole place was dark, with soft wall lighting and a big disco ball over the dance floor. Tables and chairs had been placed around the raised stage, which was set with piano, drum kit and several chairs and microphone stands.

Chloe told us that the open mike session ran from nine-thirty to eleven-thirty. "Then Jonno says they take the tables and chairs away and it turns into some middle-aged disco."

A waiter showed us to Jonno's table, right at the front by the stage. We sat down and Chloe and Ryan started chatting excitedly. The atmosphere was tense with anticipation. Loads of people were already in the room and more were flooding in.

My mind drifted to Catalina. I wondered if Ryan was right about her liking me. Probably. Ryan was rarely wrong about things like that. Knowing that she fancied me but that nothing would happen because we were both going out with other people was kind of exciting. Like a secret we shared that no-one else would ever know.

Except freakin' Ryan, of course.

Then I looked up. And saw Eve walking towards me.

And I forgot I'd ever met Catalina.

8
Open Mike Night

Eve was wearing a short, shimmery dress that clung gently to her body as she glided across the room. I couldn't take my eyes off her.

She drew closer, smiling at me. Her face was *so* beautiful. Her soft, slender body *so* naturally, effortlessly, mesmerisingly sexy. My heart pounded. What did she see in me? How was I ever going to stop some other guy from stealing her away?

As she sat down next to me, I leaned over to kiss her. She drew back sharply. And I remembered.

Jonno.

He strode up behind her, cigar in one hand. "Hi guys," he grinned. A waiter appeared at his elbow and he ordered a round of drinks. Whisky for him. Beers for us. He winked at Ryan. "Maybe something stronger later," he said. Then he strode off again.

I ground my teeth. "I've had such a shit day," I said to Eve.

"Me too," she said. "I had to spend the whole afternoon after work with Dad and Lola. She's hideous. She's twenty-three and she was all, like, 'let's be friends Evie'. That's what she called me. 'Evie'."

"Where's she from?" Ryan asked.

"California," Eve said. "Via the nearest plastic surgery clinic."

This was surprisingly bitchy for Eve. I looked at her, shocked.

"What?" she said. "She's had her nose done as well. She told me. Oh, God, Luke. She's a total cow. *And* she's the singer with the band here."

She seemed close to tears. I wanted to put my arm round her, but I didn't dare. So I leaned towards her and was about to tell her how gorgeous she was, when Jonno's voice boomed through the nightclub.

"Good evening. Good evening. And welcome to Open Mike Night at La Villa Bonita."

Jonno was speaking from the very front of the stage. An enthusiastic burst of applause followed his words, then the room fell silent again.

"The fun starts in thirty minutes. But to warm us all up, please put your hands together and welcome Band Bonita."

We clapped as a line of grey-haired men traipsed onto the stage.

Ryan caught my eye. "They rock," he said sarcastically.

"Check out the drummer," Chloe said, clapping more fervently. "Oh my God."

I strained to see past the other men to where a much younger guy was adjusting the position of the drum kit. He stood up and flicked back his black hair. He looked about seventeen or eighteen and was tall and broad-shouldered, with a strong, square-jawed face.

"Whaddya reckon, Eve? Definitely doable?" Chloe shrieked.

I glanced crossly at Eve. She caught my eye and looked away from the drummer, blushing.

Excellent.

"And, the star of the show, the amazing . . . the stupendous . . . Lola LaServa."

From behind the stage Lola appeared. She wore a skin-tight evening dress, slit up to her hip and down to her belly button. Wolf whistles and clapping filled the room. I glanced across at Ryan. He was slumped in his chair, staring at Lola, one hand on Chloe's shoulder, the other theatrically clutching at his chest.

Next to me Eve pressed her lips tightly together. I'd never seen her look so miserable. I reached under the table and squeezed her hand. She smiled weakly at me.

I didn't want to upset Eve by watching Lola sing. But, frankly, when you're in that kind of club, there isn't an awful lot you can do except watch the band. They played swing music. The older guys were surprisingly cool, strumming nonchalantly away on their guitars or sitting slumped in their chairs, blowing lazily on trumpets and horns.

The drummer looked sulky and bored, tapping and swishing at his drums. Lola herself was extraordinary. Quite apart from the fact that she appeared in constant danger of falling out of her dress, she sang in this low, sexy growl, clenching her fists and waving her arms around. It was hardly my kind of music, but I could see she was good at it.

Lola sang her way through four songs straight, then left the stage.

"She's amazing," Ryan grinned. He raised his eyebrows. "*Outstanding*, in fact."

Eve narrowed her eyes. "Let me tell you," she spat. "Those comedy boobs are the least fake thing about her."

There was an awkward pause.

"Sorry, Ry," Eve said. "I didn't mean to . . . I'm just. . ." Her eyes filled with tears.

Unable to give her a hug I felt helpless. I glanced at Chloe. She rolled her eyes at me. "Eve?" she said gently.

Eve blinked back her tears. "I'm fine." She turned to me,

clearly wanting to change the subject. "How was all your homework?"

"Gross." I remembered Mum's email. "Mum reckons she's having a boy, by the way."

Chloe squealed with excitement. "A boy? I was kind of hoping for a girl – more dolly clothes, but still, we can. . ." She stopped and glared at me. "You've known that all day and you've only just told me?"

"I don't see why it's such a big deal," I said. "It's only gonna puke and poo and scream for the first few years anyway."

Chloe slammed her glass down so hard that beer splashed out onto the tablecloth. "You insensitive retard," she said. "Just 'cause it doesn't mean anything to you."

"Doesn't it, Luke?" Eve frowned. "Don't you care about having a baby brother?"

I looked desperately at her. "Sure," I said unconvincingly. I glanced over at Ryan.

He waved me away with a look that said, *You dug your own hole there, mate.*

"You're so immature. . ." Chloe's words were cut off by the boom of Jonno's voice echoing round the room again.

"And now, the Open Mike Night begins."

Drum roll.

The table fell silent. I sat there awkwardly as the first

71

couple of people got up on stage and squawked their way through some ancient songs I didn't know.

Why was everyone so upset that I wasn't excited about Mum having a baby? I mean, the baby wasn't even a real person yet. I just didn't get it.

And why did I keep getting it wrong with Eve? I looked across to the side of the stage, where Jonno and Lola were now standing, side by side. It was their fault, I decided. Lola had somehow upset Eve, and Jonno was determined to spoil everything for both of us.

I was just about to whisper to Eve that maybe we could slip away later – no, that we *had* to slip away later – when there was a small commotion at the table and I looked round to discover Chloe making her way onto the stage.

Avoiding the grey-haired pianist who appeared to be coordinating what people were singing, Chloe marched over to the drummer and began talking to him. He smiled, then started laughing. I looked at Ryan. He was gazing tenderly at Chloe.

Then he turned and caught me watching him. "What?"

I shrugged.

"Luke's wondering why you're not jealous of Chloe talking to that guy," Eve said icily.

I looked away. That was, in fact, exactly what I'd been

thinking. Ryan stared at me. "Chloe's just having fun," he said.

The noise level in the room rose as people started chatting impatiently. The pianist strode over to Chloe and extricated her from the drummer. A minute later Chloe was singing. Some old ballad I vaguely recognised. She had an okay voice. Nothing special, but she was clearly enjoying herself so much that the audience burst into the biggest round of applause so far when she finished.

She bounded back to our table, flushed with excitement.

"That was so cool," she said. "You have to try it. Go on Ry."

She hauled a protesting Ryan to his feet. I watched him. Even as he was saying "No", he was edging closer to the band.

Give it up, Ry, I thought. *You're just as much of a show off as she is.*

"You were great, Chloe," Eve said, as Chloe took a sip from her drink.

Chloe beamed. Ryan was on stage now, chatting with the pianist. He, too, wandered over to the drummer. I watched them talking. Ryan was pointing back at Chloe, presumably explaining she was his girlfriend. I smiled. Maybe Ryan wasn't quite so immune from jealousy as he made out. Then the music struck up. It was another old swing

73

tune. God knows how Ryan knew the words. He sang terribly. Barely in tune and rasping out most of the lyrics. But the funny thing was, it didn't matter. Ryan had this way of flirting with the audience when he sang that made you forget his voice. He sauntered around the stage, pointing at people and smiling, like he was singling them out.

Chloe leaned across to me. "Isn't he fantastic?"

As the song came to an end, Ryan received a big round of applause. He flumped back down in his seat looking extremely pleased with himself. Chloe flung her arms round him and kissed him.

Jonno marched over with Lola. I kicked Chloe under the table, worried Jonno was about to tell her and Ryan off for embarrassing the guests by snogging in public. Chloe looked up as Jonno loomed over the table, beaming at us.

"Great show," he said. "Guys, this is Lola."

I felt Eve hold my hand under the table. Lola gave a bored look round. Her lips curved into a smile as her heavily made-up eyes met mine. "Hey, there," she drawled.

"Hey," I squeaked. Lola was, frankly, terrifying. Like a great big sexy snake – the sort that swallow their victims whole.

I felt Eve draw her hand away from mine. I looked at her, my face reddening.

"Thanks," she whispered, her voice low and bitter.

"What?"

"Your turn, Babycakes." Jonno grinned at Eve. "The open mike awaits you."

The table fell silent. I could feel Eve freeze beside me.

"No, Daddy," she croaked.

"Yes, Daddy." Jonno chewed on his cigar. "Come on. I want to see what I've been paying for. You've had eight months to practise."

I frowned. What was he talking about?

Eve was shrinking back in her chair. "Please don't make me," she said, in this tiny, little-girly voice. "I'm too shy."

"Don't be ridiculous." Jonno stood over Eve, a smile fixed to his lips. His presence so close was overpowering just like when he'd told me not to go anywhere near Eve.

No wonder Eve's mum was scared of him.

"You're singing, Eve. Now."

Eve stood up slowly. I could do nothing except watch as she followed Jonno onto the stage. I glanced at Chloe and Ryan. They were kissing again, oblivious to Eve's misery.

Lola slid into Eve's empty seat.

"Having fun?" She ran a long, pink nail across the table-cloth in front of me.

I nodded vaguely, all my attention on Eve.

She was standing in front of the microphone now,

looking absolutely petrified. Jonno and the pianist were standing beside her, deep in discussion. Part of me fantasised about going up there, grabbing her hand and pulling her away. But, of course, I didn't.

The music started up – a soft tune on the piano, a delicate hiss on the drums. Eve was staring down at the floor. My heart was in my mouth. Suppose she was too scared to make any sound at all?

Then she looked up, her eyes glistening, and opened her mouth. This pure, perfect sound soared round the room. Every note, every word was rich and whole, like gold melting. Or maybe it was just me? I looked round the room. No. The entire audience was on the edge of their seats, silent, eager to catch the next note. Ryan and Chloe had stopped kissing and were staring at Eve, open-mouthed. I could feel Lola beside me, also transfixed.

I looked back at Eve. She hadn't moved from the microphone and I was pretty sure she hadn't looked directly at anyone in the audience, but somehow her presence was filling the nightclub through the sad, deep, heartbreak of her song.

She finished and looked back down at the floor. There was a pause. Then the room burst into tumultuous applause. Jonno strode over to Eve and pulled her into an enormous hug. Lola got up and wandered over to them both.

The three of them talked for a minute. Then Eve was back, flushed and happy, at the table.

Chloe hugged her. "You were brilliant."

"Where did you learn to sing like that?" Ryan asked.

Eve's blush deepened. "I've been having singing lessons since February," she said. "Dad pays for them. He thinks I've got talent, but . . . it's just . . . I like singing, but not in public like this. . ." she tailed off.

I stared at her. She'd been having singing lessons since before we'd started going out? Why hadn't she ever mentioned it?

"Is the teacher a man?" I said, suspiciously.

Everyone stared at me.

"For goodness sake, Luke," Chloe said in a disgusted voice. "Is that all you ever think about?"

"She's a woman." Eve looked down at the tablecloth.

Awkward pause. Then Ryan squeezed Eve's arm. "She's obviously brilliant, whoever she is." He stared at me. "Don't you think, Luke? Didn't Eve sound fantastic?"

Eve looked up at me, her eyes all innocent and hopeful. In the heartbeat that followed, I opened my mouth. A little voice in my head was telling me just to tell her that she was great, that she'd sounded amazing, that I was so proud of her.

I ignored it.

"Why didn't you tell me you were having singing lessons?" I snapped.

Eve's mouth trembled. Then she turned and rushed out of the room.

9

Jealous guy

"You are such an idiot," Ryan said for the tenth time. "What were you thinking?"

I sat, my eyes shut, my head resting in my hands, wishing he would stop.

The evening lay in ruins.

After Eve had rushed out, Chloe had followed her. That was over half an hour ago. Now the open mike sessions were reaching their climax, and the nightclub was buzzing with excitement.

Except at our table.

Jonno and Lola were nowhere to be seen. I almost wished they would come back. Maybe it would shut Ryan up.

"Well?" he said. "What's the matter with you?"

I shook my head. I didn't know what the matter was. All

I knew was that I couldn't bear the idea of Eve doing anything with anyone I didn't know about.

"You have to stop it, man." Ryan's voice was suddenly serious. "You're going to drive her away."

I looked up at him, shocked. "D'you really think so?"

Ryan rolled his eyes. "Frankly, I'm surprised she hasn't already dumped you. You're worse than her dad."

I stared at him, stung. "I'm not anything like him. He's . . . he's—"

"Possessive and overbearing," Ryan snapped. "Just like you."

"I'm not," I protested. "I just don't like it when other guys make it obvious . . . you know. . ."

Ryan shook his head contemptuously at me.

"You don't either," I said, feeling irritated. "I saw you telling that drummer Chloe fancied that she was your girlfriend."

Ryan's face creased with exasperation. "I was telling him how we hang out at the Garito, you idiot," he said. "I was asking if he ever went there."

I stared at him. "Why? Why would you do that when you can see Chloe liked him?"

Ryan stared back at me. "Why get so heavy about it? Why's it such a big deal?"

A hand clipped the top of my head. "Ow." I spun

round. Chloe was standing behind my chair, glaring down at me.

"You are such an idiot."

I grabbed her arm. "Where's Eve?"

"She's been crying in the loo for the past thirty minutes."

I sank back in my seat.

Chloe slid into the one next to me and folded her arms. "I told her she could do miles better than you."

"Thanks, Chlo," I said bitterly. "I really app—"

"Anyway, she's gone out to the beach now, says she needs—"

But I didn't wait to hear what Eve had said she needed. I was already halfway across the nightclub floor, pushing past tables, rushing for the door. I ran across the main lobby and out past the pool, down to the beach.

My heart thudded against my chest. I had to find Eve. Apologise. Make her see how much I cared about her. Wanted her. Needed her.

I looked up and down the beach. It was another beautiful evening, a warm breeze rolling in off the sea, distant waves lapping at the sand.

There. I saw Eve about a hundred yards ahead of me, her shoes dangling from her hand.

I raced after her. I didn't call out. I was scared if I did she would run away, into the trees at the side. The beach was almost empty. Most people were still at the Open Mike Night, though a few couples were strolling along, hand in hand.

I ran up beside her. "Eve?" I said. "Eve?"

She didn't look at me, just kept walking.

I fell into step beside her. My heart was pumping so fast now I thought it might burst. "Please, Eve." My voice cracked. "I'm sorry I upset you. I don't know what's the matter with me. I just hate being here and not being able to be with you. It's . . . it's driving me crazy."

She looked up at me at last. Her face was pale in the moonlight. I could make out the tracks of her tears down her cheeks.

"You're so beautiful," I said. "And you sang so beautifully too. And I'm such an idiot."

I stopped, not knowing what else to say.

We walked along silently for a few minutes. What should I do now? I wanted just to grab her and hug her and make everything all right. But I didn't know if that's what she wanted. I reached out and felt for her hand.

I curled my fingers round hers, half expecting her to pull her hand away. She didn't. She stopped walking and looked up at me.

"Luke." Her eyes filled with tears.

Jesus. She's going to dump me.

My stomach twisted into a huge, agonising knot. I pulled her towards me and kissed her. At first I just wanted to stop her saying anything else. But then I felt her respond, her tongue soft in my mouth. And all I could think about was wanting her.

I kissed her as slowly and gently as I could, trying to do it exactly how she'd taught me, all those months ago.

She drew back and smiled up at me.

"I love the way we do that," she whispered.

I nestled my forehead down against hers and ran my fingertips down her back. She shivered and closed her eyes. I kissed her again, my hands moving lower and lower. . .

Then suddenly Eve was twisting away. I stumbled slightly on the sand.

"Luke," she said softly. "It's too easy to just . . . I mean . . . we ought to talk. Don't you think?"

"Okay." To be honest, I didn't really see what there was to talk about. Whatever had gone wrong between us was all right now, wasn't it? Still. If Eve had something on her mind I knew she wouldn't be happy until she'd talked it through.

I took her hand and we walked further up the beach.

Eve explained how she'd been too embarrassed to tell anyone about her singing lessons.

"I thought it would sound all stupid and pretentious," she

said, putting her arm round my waist. "I didn't even want to do it that much, but my dad *made* me. You know what he's like." She rested her head on my shoulder. "I don't know why I didn't say anything. It just felt like this really private thing. And I didn't want Chloe and Ryan to laugh at me or expect me to *perform* or something. And now I'm going to have to put up with Lola going on about it – she'll probably suggest we sing a duet or something. Honestly, she is *such* a bitch, she. . ."

As Eve segued into another rant about Lola, my mind drifted off, mainlining on the feel of her body next to mine.

A minute later Eve sighed. "Are you even listening to me?"

I jumped guiltily. "Of course." I looked round. We had wandered way past the staff cabins and the Garito. The beach was completely deserted up here. "Why don't we sit down for a bit?" I said.

I pulled Eve over to the trees at the top of the beach and smoothed out a patch of sand for her. "Sorry I haven't got anything for you to sit on," I mumbled.

She smiled at me. "'S okay." She sat down beside me and looked out at the sea, her arms wrapped round her knees.

We were silent for what felt like a long time. Then Eve leaned back and put her hands on the sand beside her.

"I hate the way I look," she said.

I stared at her. The moon was shining on her hair, lighting the side of her face. She was, without doubt, the best-looking person I'd ever met. "But you look amazing," I frowned. "You're . . . you're beautiful."

She smiled sadly at me. "That's what I mean." She paused, scrunching a handful of sand between her fingers. "It's like . . . like being pretty is all anyone ever sees. No-one sees *me*. Who I am."

I reached out for her hand. "I do," I said.

Eve gazed at my hand on top of hers. She pulled hers away and let the sand run out from between her fingers. "Do you?" she said, dully.

"Yes." I scrambled onto my knees, eager to prove it.

"How do I feel about my dad, then?" she asked.

"Um . . . well . . . you love him, obviously, because he's your dad." I paused, trying to work it out. "But he also annoys you, like with the singing thing and 'cause he's weird with you about boys and stuff."

Eve shook her head and stared out to sea. "I adore my dad," she said. "I always have. When I was little I couldn't wait for him to come and take me out. I wouldn't be able to sleep the night before, I'd be so excited. And then sometimes he wouldn't make it and I'd get so upset." She paused and when she spoke again her voice was practically a whisper. "When he did come, it was always so fantastic. He was so handsome and he'd take me out and buy me stuff and make me feel like a princess. *His* princess. Like the most special person in the world."

I looked from her to the sea, stretched out in front of us like a soft, dark blanket.

Eve sighed. "But when I got older I realised that he didn't see who I was at all. He doesn't want me to grow up and have a life. He just wants me to stay his little Babycakes. Only there for him to look at and show off. And, as far as I can see, that's what all guys want." Eve's voice wobbled. "They don't care who you are, just so long as you look hot and their friends are impressed."

"That's not me," I said. "That was Ben, maybe, but. . ."

"Then why d'you get so jealous all the time?" Eve started sobbing, her voice all broken and small. "Why can't you see how I feel about you? Why don't you trust me?"

I couldn't bear seeing her cry. I hugged her, stroking her hair. "I *do* trust you," I said. "It's the other guys I don't trust."

Eve pulled away from me, wiping her face. She smiled exasperatedly at me. "God, Luke. That's *exactly* what my dad says."

"Okay," I said. "I'll change. I'll stop being jealous. I promise." I pulled her towards me again.

"EVE!" Jonno's voice bellowed in the distance.

Eve sprang away from me. She scrambled to her feet.

"Quick. Go." She pointed to the woods behind us. "Hide there until he's gone."

I stood up and grabbed her hand. "No," I said. "We're not doing anything wrong. Why should I hide?"

Eve's eyes widened. "He'll kill you if he finds you out here with me."

The sensible part of me was pretty sure she was right. Or close enough to it. But I was angry. "He's got no right to tell you that you can't see me. Why don't we just go and tell him we're going out together?"

Eve looked at me as if I was mad.

"EVE!" Jonno's voice was getting closer.

Eve wrenched her hand out of mine.

"What are you so frightened of?" I whispered, suddenly seeing it in her eyes. "I mean he might be pissed off to start with, but there's nothing he can he actually *do* about us being together, is there?"

Eve blinked at me, then turned and ran rapidly along the beach.

I flumped down on the sand, watching her disappear behind the line of trees.

"There you are, Babycakes." Jonno's voice – part angry, part relieved – grated on my nerves. "I was worried about you. I don't like you coming out this far by yourself."

She wasn't by herself. I was here. I was looking after her.

Eve said something quickly I couldn't catch.

"That's what I wanted to talk to you about," Jonno said. "I want you to sing every night. Just a couple of numbers, when Lola takes her breaks."

I froze. No way. Eve and I were already separated in the mornings and afternoons. The old bastard couldn't do this.

"It'll be good for you – build your confidence," Jonno went on. "And it'll give you something to do while you're here."

You mean give her even less time to enjoy herself. With me.

"But Daddy, I was so scared." Eve's voice rose to a squeak. "I don't think I can."

"Don't be ridiculous, Babycakes. You sounded fantastic. Everybody said so. I talked to the band. They reckon you need a bit of work on the performance side of things, but you've got all the raw materials. Lola's done a song-list for you to choose some songs from. Here."

I heard the sound of paper rustling. *Tell him, Eve. Tell him "no".*

But in my heart I knew it was hopeless.

As their voices drifted out of earshot I heard her little-girly voice, all anxious and eager to please: "Okay, Daddy. Okay, if that's what you want. Of course I will."

I flung myself back on the sand and thumped it, hard.

10

The baby magnet

I woke the next morning to find Ryan prodding my shoulder.

"What?" I said, irritably.

"Up," he said. "We're on pool duty, nine till eleven."

I groaned and sat up. "What time is it now?"

"Five to nine."

"What?" I scrambled out of bed and reached for my shorts. "Why didn't you wake me earlier?"

"Who am I – your mother?" Ryan grinned at me. "You make up with Eve, then?"

Last night flooded back. After Eve had left I'd stayed on the beach a long time, falling asleep and waking up cold much later.

"I think so."

Ryan sniffed at a T-shirt, then pulled it on over his head.

"You missed a great night at the Garito. Catalina asked where you were. And Alejandro was there too."

"Who's Alejandro?" I said, trying to copy the way Ryan pronounced the "j" as an exaggerated "h".

"The drummer from the band – remember? He's cool – loads of money, but doesn't flash it around. His dad's one of Eve's dad's business partners. That's why he's here, playing in the band. But he's really into rock music. He's going on tour with some Spanish group when he's finished here."

"Sounds like he really opened up to you," I stuck my head under the cold tap in the bathroom. "D'you think you'll kiss on the second date?"

"Piss off." Ryan appeared in the bathroom doorway, grinning. "Chloe did most of the talking. I just stood there, chatting up all the hot girls who were hanging around hoping Alejandro'd speak to them."

A minute later and we were out the door and racing round to the pool. Jonno was already out there, cigar clamped between his lips.

He pointed to his watch as we ran up. "You're late."

"Sorry, sir," Ryan panted. "Won't happen again."

"Make sure it doesn't," Jonno growled.

We set out the loungers and sun umbrellas. Soon the pool area was full of small kids with their parents, splashing and yelling in the water.

Catalina turned up half an hour into the shift. She went straight over to Jonno, who was leaning against the pool bar, drinking a cup of coffee.

I looked up, expecting to see him shouting at her for being late, but to my surprise they were laughing together.

"How come she doesn't get told off?" I said to Ryan as we sorted through the dirty pool towels. "She's way later than we were."

Ryan gave me a withering look. "Why d'you think?"

Catalina skipped towards us with a smile.

"Where are you last night?" she pouted up at me. "You said you come to El Garito."

I smiled uneasily. "Fell asleep on the beach," I said.

Catalina brushed past me, reaching for the pile of clean towels. She put her hand on my arm to steady herself. "Mmmn," she said, squeezing above my elbow. "Nice muskells."

Ryan snorted as Catalina wiggled off down the side of the pool, towels in her arms. "One day, that girl is gonna get sooo busted," he said.

I watched her lean over and take a drinks order from one of the sunbathers.

"You're just jealous 'cause it's my muskells she likes," I grinned.

But inside my head, in a part of my brain completely

91

separate from how I felt about Eve, I couldn't help imagining what it would be like to kiss her.

Eve didn't appear all morning and she didn't reply to my texts. After pool duty finished, I wandered around for about thirty minutes, looking for her. Eventually I gave up and went to do my homework in the unairconditioned broom cupboard. It was even hotter and noisier than yesterday.

I struggled with some maths questions on probability, then – deciding I deserved a break – checked out my emails. There was another message from Mum.

Dear Luke. Not sure if you got my last email. Here's the early scan of the baby. All healthy as far as they can tell. It's too soon to know, but I'm sure it's a boy! Lots and lots of love to everyone, Mum.

I clicked on the attachment. A fuzzy, black and white photograph flashed onto the screen. I stared at it for a few minutes but couldn't, for the life of me, work out any part of it that remotely resembled human life. Remembering how annoyed Chloe had been at me yesterday, though, I printed it out and shoved it in my pocket.

Pushing away thoughts of Dad and how he would feel about the baby, I sent an email back to Mum saying how pleased Chloe and I were that everything was okay.

See? I'm not completely insensitive.

I ploughed on with the next load of maths, a series of immensely complicated and incredibly boring equations. My head grew heavy. In fact, I was almost asleep on the keyboard when Ryan and Marco barged in.

"Brought you some lunch." Ryan shoved a slice of dried-up pizza under my nose.

I showed Marco and Ryan the baby scan.

"Can you work out where its head is?" I said, my mouth full of pizza.

Ryan pointed to a dark curve in the bottom left of the picture. "Maybe that?" he said.

"I thought that was its bum," I said.

"No. That it pee-pee place," Marco said.

We all laughed.

Ryan and Marco stayed for about ten minutes. I was half listening to their conversation, half working on my equations, when the sound of girls giggling nearby drifted in from outside.

Our heads turned together to look out through the window.

Most of the female staff seemed to be gathered on the grass at the near end of the pool, along with a smattering of teenage-girl hotel guests. A lone male, dressed only in swimming trunks, stood in their midst.

"That's Alejandro," Ryan said, delightedly.

I peered at him. The sulky drummer of last night had gone. In his place was a tall, smiling guy with a tan and a six-pack.

I grimaced. "Looks a bit full of himself."

"That's the funny thing," Ryan said. "He looks the way he does *and* he's loaded and yet he's totally sound."

"Is true," Marco said. "I know Alejandro only since few weeks. He is . . . how you say . . . a baby magnet."

"Babe magnet," Ryan corrected him.

"*Si*. Babe magnet. But he very respectful with girls. Nice guy. Everyone like him."

"Has he got a girlfriend?" I asked.

Marco shrugged. "*No se*. I don't know. But he never push with girls. And they all like it. I think even my Catalina like him."

I caught Ryan's eye and felt myself reddening. My phone rang and I bent over the text. It was from Eve, saying she was going to have to spend the afternoon rehearsing with the band.

"Great."

Ryan peered at the text over my shoulder. "Well, why don't you go and watch?" he said.

I looked through the window to where the band's good-looking and apparently unattached drummer was still chatting and joking with the girls outside.

Forgetting my promise to Eve not to be jealous any more, I decided that watching her rehearsal was the best way of keeping an eye on both her and Alejandro.

"Good idea," I said, flipping shut my phone. "I think I will."

11

Rehearsal

The rehearsal was not going well. Eve had spent hours practising the first two songs on the list Jonno had given her, but the pianist – the grey-haired leader of the band – was not satisfied. He kept exploding into rapid-fire Spanish and stomping round the stage waving his arms theatrically in Eve's direction.

"He says you must look at the audience more," Alejandro said.

Alejandro.

It was horribly clear to me that, without him, Eve would be having a far worse time than she was. For a start, he translated everything the irate pianist said into perfect English for her. On top of that, he repeatedly told her she sounded good *and* he appeared to be the main reason why the rest of the band didn't get bored with the constant stoppages. He laughed and joked with them in Spanish whenever the pianist brought the music to a standstill.

None of this, of course, made me like him.

The rehearsals took place in the nightclub. This looked rather drab and dirty by daylight, all scuffed wooden floor and stained, brown sofas. The air con made it feel even bleaker. I was sitting at a scratched metal table near the back. Without its white tablecloth and candles, it looked like a camping table.

"Or like Lola without her make-up," Eve said, bitterly, in one of the short breaks the pianist had given her.

Lola herself turned up about halfway through the rehersal. She had what looked like a furious row in Spanish with the pianist, then came and flung herself down beside me.

I squirmed uneasily as she leaned closer.

"You like the music?" she drawled.

I shrugged, trying not to stare at her chest. Close to it was impossible not to notice – it filled almost all the available space in my field of vision.

"Or maybe you like singers?" Lola lingered on the "s", placing her hand on the back of my chair. I fixed my eyes on her face. Hard, black-ringed eyes. Red, pouty lips. She was like a cartoon of someone hot – utterly fake. Absolutely terrifying. And deeply, sluttily sexy.

"I see you like *this* singer." Lola nodded towards Eve on the stage.

I shrugged, trying to look nonchalant about it.

"Though her father still seems to think she's a little girl unable to cope with real life." Lola gave a contemptuous sniff. "Still, he'll learn, won't he?"

Without waiting for me to reply, she strode off to the stage and started shouting in Spanish at the pianist again.

Eve walked over, frowning. "What did *she* want?"

"I have no idea," I said, honestly. "Er . . . Alejandro seems nice."

Eve's frown vanished. She beamed at me. "I thought so, too. Oh, Luke, I'm so pleased you said that. I was really worried you'd be all jealous about him because. . ." She stopped.

"Because he's so horny?" I said, forcing a smile onto my face. "Yeah, I noticed everyone round here seems to think he's all that. But why should I worry? You're with me, right?"

I was rewarded for this speech with an even bigger smile. Eve leaned towards me, her hair brushing against my face. "I so want to kiss you," she said.

"*Eva. Eva. Ven aquí,*" barked the pianist. Lola was flouncing out through the back of the stage. Alejandro waved at us, beckoning Eve back.

"Later?" I said, raising my eyebrows.

"Later." Eve went back to the stage and sang both her songs again. This time she looked straight at me while she was singing. It was kind of nice. Like she was singing for me.

Afterwards, even the pianist seemed satisfied.

Ryan and Chloe appeared while the band were packing up.

"Free time for the rest of the day," Ryan grinned. "We're going into Cala del Toro for a beer. D'you two wanna come?"

Eve looked across at Alejandro, who was still talking to the pianist.

"We could ask Alejandro?" Ryan said.

"Yum," Chloe said enthusiastically.

Eve turned to me. "What d'you think, Luke?"

I stared into her pale blue eyes.

No. No. No. I want to be alone with you. I don't want to go for a drink with everyone else. And certainly not with Mr Freakin' Perfect with his drums and his abs and his everyone-loves-me smile.

"Good idea," I said. "Why don't you ask him."

We sauntered up the road to Cala del Toro at about five o'clock. It was still hot, but the deliciously sweet breeze stopped the air from being suffocating. Ryan and Chloe strolled hand in hand but, as usual, Eve and I were careful to walk slightly apart from each other in case anyone from the hotel saw us.

Not that Eve seemed to mind. She chatted happily to Alejandro as we wandered away from the shore, up to the square in the middle of town. The tables belonging to the cafes round the outside of the stone plaza were mostly empty and the central area was quiet too – just a couple of old men arguing over a dominoes game at a little iron table, and a small group of Spanish kids playing tag.

We sat at a round, cast-iron table outside a cafe, in the shade of a cluster of olive trees. Alejandro knew one of the waiters and they talked briefly in Spanish while Eve and I held hands under the table.

After an hour in his company I had to admit that Alejandro was, like Ryan had said, a sound guy. He was eighteen, but didn't seem to mind in the slightest that we were all younger than him. He was clearly massively well off – even I could see his clothes were expensive – and his wallet was stuffed with euros. He paid for everything. He insisted. And yet he did it in this easy-going way that never made you feel uncomfortable about it.

"It is my treat for pushing into your drink," he said, flashing a smile round at all of us. And that was another thing. He didn't get all sexed-up over the girls. He was just nice. As nice to me and Ryan as he was to Eve and Chloe.

"I only play in the band to please my father," he explained to me in his lightly accented, rather formal English. "It is our deal. I will work for him over the summer and he will let me follow my dream after." He rolled his eyes. "It would be better to follow my dream now, but still. . ." He smiled at Eve. ". . .you know fathers."

Then he turned to me. "Is yours the same?"

I stared at him. "Mine's dead," I said.

Alejandro looked stricken. "I am so sorry." He glanced over at Chloe. "How stupid I feel . . . I. . ."

"It's okay. It's okay," we kept saying.

Chloe went on, trying to reassure him. In the end I sat back, embarrassed at how red-faced Alejandro had become.

I hadn't let myself think about Dad properly for ages. I mean, he came into my head several times a day – memories and stuff like that. But I hadn't really let myself imagine him or what it might be like to actually speak to him – not for a long time. Right now I did, though. It occurred to me I could have asked him what *he* thought I should feel about Mum having a baby with Matt.

And about Eve, about how to deal with other guys liking her.

As the light began to fade, I noticed Alejandro look at Eve several times, but the only sign that he might have anything more than friendship on his mind came right at the end of our drink, when Chloe asked him how come his English was so good.

"I was taught by a private tutor." Alejandro grimaced. "My father thinks everyone must speak English to succeed in business. He still thinks I might want to be in business, for some reason." He smiled. "I remember my tutor makes me . . . I mean *made* me, play this game with words to help with English pronunciation. A rhyming game. So he gave me a word and I told him a word it rhymes with. Then he made me do it with names. It is very hard."

"Do it with my name," Chloe demanded. "Go on."

Alejandro's eyes twinkled. "Chloe . . . Chloe . . . glowy. Like the candles and fire. Glowy."

Chloe grinned. "What about 'Ryan'?"

Ryan laughed. "That's too hard. Do 'Ry'."

Alejandro smiled. "Easy: try, why, fry, high, sigh. . ."

"I know a rhyme for 'Ryan'," Eve said softly. "Cyan."

"What's that?" Alejandro said.

"It's a colour. Blue." Eve blushed, like she always did when she thought she might be seen as showing off about something.

Alejandro didn't take his eyes off her. "'Eve' is easy," he

said. "Eve. Believe. Never leave." He caught my eye and sat up straighter. "Then 'Luke'."

"Don't bother with me," I said hastily. "I've been hearing it since I was seven. Luke. Puke."

Alejandro raised his eyes. "What is 'puke'? I was going to say fluke. Which is how you got a beautiful girl like Eve. No?"

Eve breathed in sharply. I stared at him, my heart thudding. He knew about me and Eve? But we'd been careful. All evening all we'd done was hold hands once – and that only under the table.

I glanced at Eve. Her face was white, her eyes scared.

"Alejandro," she said. "My dad. . ."

"I know. It is okay. I will no say anything."

"How did you know?" Eve said.

Alejandro gazed at her, a slow smile curling round his mouth. "The way you sang to him. The way he has looked at you all evening."

I stared at him. Alejandro was still smiling at Eve.

"We should go back," he said. "We are supposed to be back at the nightclub for nine and you have to get ready in your beautiful dress."

She stood up.

"I'll come too," I said.

Alejandro shook his head. "There is no need for you to do that," he said. "I will look after your girl."

Eve rolled her eyes. "Excuse me," she said. "I don't need looking after." She leaned down and whispered in my ear. "You stay here for a bit," she said. "I don't go on for the first half an hour and you know you don't really like the music."

I nodded, hating the fact that if I said I wanted to go back with her now she would just think I was being jealous.

I watched them walk off together, an uneasy feeling in the pit of my stomach.

12

Missing Eve

Over the next week Eve spent more time with Alejandro than she did with me. It wasn't anyone's fault. Apart from Jonno's, of course.

Anyway, what with my homework, our separate work shifts and her having to spend large portions of the afternoon and evening hanging around for rehearsals and performances, there were some days when we hardly saw each other.

Alejandro, on the other hand, had no calls on his time other than the same rehearsals and performances Eve was involved in. He helped her a lot. He kept the temperamental pianist away as much as he could and he gave her advice and encouragement the whole time.

That first night, Eve was so nervous I thought she was going to be sick. She was standing backstage in her shimmery dress, clutching her stomach and shaking.

"Why is my Dad making me do this?" she wailed. "I can't do it. Not with all those people watching. I can't remember the words. I can't remember when to come in. I can't do it."

I stared at her, my heart pounding, not knowing what to say.

Alejandro gripped her shoulders. "You know the song, Eva," he said. "Just do it like earlier. If you forget your cues the band will follow you. If you forget the words, sing 'la, la, la' or the last verse over again. And smile. Smile at the audience. Especially in the bridge. Do no forget. They *want* to like you."

Jonno gave her a big introduction. He was very clever with it. He made sure the audience didn't expect a professional – spinning this big line about Eve helping him out and hoping they wouldn't mind hearing her for just one song.

Eve got through it okay. She always sounded good to me. But when she came off stage it was Alejandro she turned to – his praise meant the most and his suggestions for improving were what she wanted to hear.

I hated it. But there was nothing I could do. I never once saw Alejandro look at or speak to Eve like he was was interested. And yet I was sure he must be. How could any guy *not* be?

After a couple of days I suggested that Eve stopped doing her other jobs, in the crèche and waiting tables.

"Surely your dad must realise how hard you're working with the band?"

Eve shook her head. "I can't stop. I'm the boss's daughter. No-one will talk to me if they think I'm arsing about, not working."

I frowned. "But what about me? I never see you."

Eve snapped that I was being selfish. "It's not easy for me," she said. "Why don't you understand? Alejandro does."

Things got worse when Alejandro's dad turned up for a few days. He and Jonno had long business meetings every evening, then took Eve, Alejandro and Lola out for late meals. For three nights I didn't see Eve at all after her nine-thirty and ten-thirty songs at the nightclub.

I went to the Garito with Ryan and Chloe. I chatted to Marco and his friends. I even got into some harmless flirting with Catalina. She'd developed this jokey habit of running her hands through my hair and saying it was getting blonder and blonder in the sun. Which it was. Then she'd give it this playful little tug and narrow her eyes in that hard, sexy way of hers. It was fun.

But even while I was soaking up Catalina's attention, Eve was always at the back of my mind. She and

Alejandro never got back from the meals out with their dads until about two a.m., when Jonno made Eve go straight up to bed. In some ways that was the worst time for me. I knew Alejandro had a room in the main part of the hotel, near the private apartment where Eve was staying with Chloe and her dad and Lola. Eve couldn't go through the lobby towards my room without the overnight receptionists seeing her. But there was nothing to stop her sneaking unnoticed into Alejandro's room in the middle of the night.

But what could I do?

I'd promised not to be jealous. And although I broke that promise every minute of every day, I couldn't let her know it.

On the fourth morning after Alejandro's dad came to visit, I checked that Jonno was by the pool, then marched up to Eve's room.

She looked anxious when she saw me.

"This isn't a good idea, Luke." She gave me a quick hug then stepped away. "What if my dad comes back. . .?"

"Screw him," I said. "It's not fair. Tonight you have to tell him you don't want to go out. Say you're ill or something. Anything."

Eve bit her lip. "I can't. But Alejandro's dad'll be gone in a couple of days. Things'll get easier then."

I pulled her towards me. "Don't you *want* to see me?"

"Of course I do." She hugged me again, resting her head on my shoulder.

We stood there for a minute. It was so good to feel her against me, her body all warm and soft and curvy. I breathed in the lemony smell of her hair, then leaned down and kissed her neck.

She tilted her head back. Seconds later we were snogging furiously, our hands everywhere. Suddenly I was off my head with wanting her. I started backing her towards the bed, loving the way she was tugging at my T-shirt, pulling me after her.

The bedroom door clicked open.

We both whipped round.

Chloe was standing there, her arms folded, a disapproving look on her face. "Ryan's just called me. He says Jonno's in reception and could be up here any minute."

I groaned. "Can't I say I'm visiting you? You're my *sister* for God's sake."

"Then you'll have to come next door into my room and actually visit me, won't you?" Chloe said, tartly. "And I'm not sitting there like some anti-chaperone watching you two grope each other to death."

I turned to Eve. "What are your shifts today?"

"Pool duty in half an hour," she said. "Then you have to

do homework and I have rehearsals and then crèche with Chloe from four to six."

I clenched my jaw. "And I'm in the restaurant from six to eight."

"Which is when I have to get ready for the nightclub." Eve sighed. "God, I hate singing in that pigging place."

"So we have half an hour now." I slid my hands down her back. "Why don't we go down to the beach?"

Eve looked up at me. "Because it takes fifteen minutes to get far enough away to be sure no-one from the hotel will see us, so as soon we get there, I'll have to come back."

She stroked my face with her fingers. I closed my eyes.

"Hel-lo," Chloe called from the door. "I strongly suggest you two tear yourselves away from each other. Now. After what Jonno did to that guy last night I would think you—"

"What guy?" I said.

Eve blushed. "It wasn't anything. Just someone at the restaurant we went to. He was drunk. He tried to . . . sort of . . . grab me when I was going to the loo. . ."

"*What?*" I stared at her. "What happened?"

"My dad punched him." Eve looked at the floor. "If Alejandro and his dad hadn't pulled him off, he'd have—"

"Guys." Chloe's voice was urgent now. "Luke, you really should leave."

I blinked, my head whirling with an anger that spiked in

110

several directions at once – at whoever had laid a hand on Eve, at Jonno for being the one who was able to punch him, at Alejandro for just being there.

Then I had an idea.

"Swap shifts with me, Chlo," I said.

She frowned.

"I'll do your crèche shift, you do my table-waiting. That way Eve and I'll be working together from four to six and free together from six till eight."

"Yes," Eve breathed excitedly. "Go on, Chloe," she urged. "We'll say Luke's covering 'cause you're sick."

Chloe shook her head at us. "Luke won't last five minutes in the crèche," she said. "But okay. If it'll get you out of here now. Yes. I'll do it."

I grinned at her, then raced down the corridor and out into the main part of the hotel. I passed Jonno on the stairs, his head bent over a bundle of papers. He didn't notice me.

Yes. I'd have loads of time with Eve this afternoon. The crèche was bound to have somewhere we could sneak off to. After all, how hard could looking after a bunch of little kids bc?

13

The crèche

Pilar, the crèche manager, was scandalised when I showed up on the doorstep instead of Chloe.

She looked me up and down, then shrieked. "But you are boy."

"So?" I said. "That's sex discrimination. There's no reason I shouldn't work here."

Pilar clutched the bunch of long chains that hung round her neck. She was tiny – her head only came up to my chest. Looking down, I could see several grey strands streaking out from the centre parting of her long black hair.

"You do no understand," she said. "The English mamas and papas do not like the boys looking after the children."

"But Chloe's not well," I lied. "I'm her brother. I'm used to kids. I have a little brother, almost."

"Very well," Pilar said with a resigned sigh. She twisted her chains round her fingers. "But you must have to stay indoors."

"Fine," I grinned. Indoors sounded good to me. Indoors sounded private.

I followed Pilar inside. The crèche was a long, low building set between the pool on one side and the trees that led down to the beach on the other. Most of the kids – aged from three to seven years, Pilar said – were outside in the playground. Two hotel workers I vaguely recognised from the Garito were out there already, pushing them on swings and spinning them on the roundabout. I wondered where Eve was. Late probably, as usual.

Pilar showed me round inside. There was a small office area with three doors off it. "Store room, bathroom and indoor play," Pilar said, pointing to each in turn.

She opened the door to the indoor play area. It was a large room with kids' drawings and paintings on every bit of wall. About fifteen children were inside. Most were sitting round the series of low tables that filled one corner. A few were being read to by a hotel staffer on the rug under the long window. There was a big sink, lots of painting stuff. . .

Through the window, I watched Eve flying past the playground. She appeared seconds later, panting, in the doorway. "Sorry I'm late Pilar. Can I be inside today?" She grinned at me.

Pilar sniffed and muttered something in Spanish. "No. Outside. We have already three in here."

I looked round. I'd only noticed one other worker – the one reading to the kids. I peered past the low table cluttered with colouring things, past the cluster of small children – to a girl at the furthest end of the table.

She looked up, narrowed her eyes and smiled at me. Catalina.

"Go with Catalina, Luke," Pilar said briskly. "She show you what to do. Vamos, Eva. Outside."

"See you later," Eve said with a little frown.

I nodded, feeling slightly uncomfortable. Pilar and Eve left. I wandered over to Catalina. One of the children – a little girl – grabbed my arm.

"I'm Saffron," she said. "I got a pony for my birthday."

"Oh?" I sat down on one of the tiny chairs. My legs bunched awkwardly. I stared at Catalina. She was wearing a Bonita Babe T-shirt that looked at least two sizes too small, even on her petite body.

She gave me a long, sexy look. "Don't worry," she said. "We do painting now. Keep them busy."

I helped her fetch the paints from the cupboard under the sink and pour them into trays. The other girl carried on reading to her small group on the mat, but the rest of the children crowded round me and Catalina, talking and shoving each other. Catalina slapped paper down on the table and told the kids to press their hands into the paint trays, then make hand prints on the paper. It was hard getting them all started, then exhausting stopping them from covering themselves with paint. In the end, Catalina made this impatient flicking gesture with her fingers.

"*Mierda*," she said. "Who care if there is mess."

The kids shrieked with excitement as Catalina encouraged them to do whatever they wanted. Two of the boys started flicking paint at each other and within half a minute the rest of the children had joined in.

Soon there were great paint splashes all over the tables, the floor and the kids. And us. After about ten minutes I stood back, staring down at my Bonita Boy T-shirt. It was so covered in red paint you could hardly see the blue of the material underneath.

Catalina sidled up to me. "You no normal working in crèche," she said, pressing her hand against what remained of the word "Bonita".

"No." I watched, mesmerised by her stretched-out fingers. She slowly smeared the paint lower, over the word "Boy". *Jesus.* Did she have any idea how much that was turning me on? I glanced guiltily towards the window. Where was Eve? "Er . . . my sister is ill," I stammered. "I'm doing her shift."

"*Si?*" Catalina stared at me with mocking brown eyes, her hand now pressed against my stomach. "Is true?"

I stared at her. Did she know about me and Eve?

The two boys who'd started flicking paint about earlier were now chucking whole handfuls of the stuff at each other. Catalina turned round and shouted something at them in Spanish. Although the children were English and, like me, couldn't have understood what she said, the meaning was clear enough. They stopped instantly.

Catalina turned back to me. She put her paint-stained hand on my upper arm. "Is good idea," she said. "Marco never come to crèche."

My eyes widened. *Oh my God. She thinks I've come here to be with her.*

The kids behind Catalina started fighting with the paint again. With a great crash one of the trays fell to the floor. Paint splashed everywhere. I backed away.

"I'll go to the store room," I said. "Find a moth. I mean a mop."

I glanced out of the window again as I walked past. Eve was out there, standing next to Pilar by the slide. She saw me and waved.

I strode into the store room, shut the door, then leaned against it.

Why hadn't it occurred to me that Catalina might be here? If Eve'd seen her coming onto me like that she'd think I'd been enouraging her. Which I had, I supposed, up at the Garito, but. . .

I took a deep breath. It was okay. Eve hadn't seen. And Cat and I hadn't actually done anything. She'd just got the wrong idea. All I had to do now was go back out and tell her about Chloe being ill again. Make it clear I hadn't come here for her.

I spotted a mop and bucket in the corner and walked towards them. The buckct was wedged between the wall and a tall cupboard, the mop stored inside it. As I yanked out the buckct, the mop fell to the floor.

It masked the sound of the door opening behind me.

I squatted down to pick up thc mop. As I pulled it upright, I felt a hand on my back. For a second I imagined it was Eve, following me inside. I turned round, smiling.

Catalina was standing over me, her lips slightly partcd.

My smile faded. I stood up awkwardly, still holding the mop, squashed in between the wall and the bucket and Cat herself.

Catalina gazed at me for a few seconds, her chocolatey

eyes hard and sexy. Then she reached up and took my face in her hands.

I gasped as she dragged her thumb across my lips.

She moved a little closer.

My heart raced. I took a small step back, knocking my heels against the bucket. I gripped the mop more tightly. "What're you doing?" I croaked. "Someone could . . . er . . . I . . . someone. . ."

Catalina curled her lip. "Marco no here."

She took another small step towards me. My feet were right up against the bucket, my fingers glued to the mop.

I leaned backwards away from her. "But," I said, hoarsely. "But . . . but. . ." I couldn't form the words. I couldn't tear my eyes from Catalina's face.

She was right there. Right up next to me, her body all compact and curvy and. . .

Catalina pressed herself against me. She smelled of dry, spicy perfume. "Only we are looking for the mop," she murmured.

She curled her fingers round my neck, running them up through my hair. Then slowly, insistently, she pulled my head down towards hers.

I was so close. Breathing in her breath. My body shaking. Right next to her mouth. . .

"*Mierda*." Pilar's voice hissed along the corridor outside.

I pushed Catalina away from me, just as the door opened. Pilar strode in.

Even though we were not now actually touching, it was obvious what had been happening. I could feel my face was bright red. I self-consciously ran my hands over my hair, smoothing it down where I imagined Cat must have ruffled it.

Pilar's tiny face was screwed up in fury. She pointed at me. "*Vete!*" she yelled. "Get out. I knowed boy bad news. *Vete! Ahora!* Go. Now."

I dropped the mop. It clattered to the floor as I scrambled past Catalina, past Pilar and into the corridor. I fled out of the crèche door, through the playground outside and up towards the side of the hotel where Ryan and I were staying. I caught sight of Eve out of the corner of my eye. But I didn't stop. I ran hard all the way back to the room. A single thought kept running through my head. If Pilar hadn't come in when she did, I would have kissed Catalina properly. I knew I would. And I knew that Cat knew it. And I was pretty sure Pilar did too.

I sat down on the bed, my head in my hands, praying that Pilar hadn't gone straight outside and told Eve.

By the time Eve turned up an hour later I had totally convinced myself she would know everything and forgive none of it. I was beside myself. How could I have been so stupid? Eve had been there. Right outside. She could have been the one who'd walked in. I'd risked losing her for what? One kiss?

A kiss I didn't even end up having.

I was so caught up in my thoughts I didn't hear the rap on the door at first. Then the knock came again, louder. I strode, miserably, across the room.

Eve was outside, still in her Bonita Babe T-shirt. She looked serious. Concerned. "I came straight round as soon as the shift finished."

I couldn't face her. I turned and walked back across the room.

"Luke?" she said.

"Nothing happened." The words burst out of me. "I didn't do anything. I swear. Whatever Pilar said."

Eve walked round in front of me. "Are you okay?" she said.

I looked at her. Why was she asking if I was okay? "What *did* Pilar say?"

Eve grinned. "That she found you in the store room with Catalina."

"I didn't do anything," I pleaded again. "Honestly. I wouldn't. I—"

Eve laughed. "I know that, you idiot." She shook her

head. "Pilar knows what Cat's like. Everyone does. All the girls here say she's got a total rep for always horning after everyone. She was bound to try it on with you." She smiled coyly up at me. "Loads of the girls here fancy you."

I frowned. "So you're not cross?"

Eve's smile broadened. She pulled me down onto the bed and cupped my face in her hands. "You're so sweet," she said. "I know you would never, ever, do anything behind my back like that. Just like I wouldn't to you."

I stared at her, suddenly feeling like the biggest bastard in the world. I knew in my heart that if no-one had disturbed us, that if I hadn't been scared of someone coming in, I would have gone as far as I could with Catalina. Not because I liked her better than Eve. I didn't. But because she was there, wanting me. Because she was hot. And because – if I was honest – it wouldn't have occurred to me to stop.

Eve stretched out on the bed. "We've got two hours now, remember?" She drew me down beside her, her fingers cool and smooth on my guilty cheeks.

My stomach twisted. I didn't deserve her. She was so good. So sweet. She didn't even suspect me of fancying Catalina. Let alone acting on it. I reached out and took her face in my hands.

All I could think was how lucky I was to have her. How close I'd come to losing her.

Losing Eve.

I could never, ever let that happen.

"I love you," I said, softly. "I see who you are. Who you *really* are, underneath how beautiful you look. And I really, really love you."

Eve blinked at me. Neither of us had ever said those words before. They'd always seemed so distant, so grown up. I mean you love your mum and dad and maybe other people in your family. But loving a girl. Being in love. It was like one minute I had no idea what that was about. And the next, I understood exactly what it meant. Because it was exactly how I felt.

We lay there, looking at each other, for a long time. Then almost as if we were reading each other's mind, we moved closer together and kissed – a deep, slow, magical kiss, that somehow shut out the rest of the world and yet contained everything we could ever need.

14

The truth about Jonno

We made out – all slow and gentle. Not the whole way, of course. Clothes on. Nothing that heavy.

Just how Eve liked it.

Me? I liked it too. I mean, sure – it was frustrating as well. But right then, I didn't care. I loved her. She loved me. And, for the first time since we'd met, I was certain that everything else was going to happen.

Soon.

I could feel it in the way she kissed me.

Half an hour later, Ryan found us, still lying stretched out beside each other on the bed. "Hi," he said. "Hey, Eve. Your dad's looking everywhere for you."

"What time is it?" Eve said, not taking her eyes from my face.

"Six-forty or so," Ryan answered. I could see him, over

Eve's shoulder, peeling off his white waiting-shirt. "I've just had the busiest tea in the history of the world. Marco and I were on our own serving about four trillion guests."

At the mention of Marco's name I felt a jolt of guilt. I wondered if he'd heard about what had happened with Catalina earlier?

"Why does my dad want me now?" Eve said, grumpily. "I'm not supposed to be anywhere until eight."

I leaned over and kissed her shoulder. Across the room, Ryan was unzipping his black trousers.

"Hey," I called. "D'you mind not stripping in front of my girlfriend?"

Ryan rolled his eyes at me, but picked up a pair of shorts and a T-shirt from the pile on the floor and strolled over to the bathroom.

Eve snuggled back down next to me.

Seconds later the bathroom door banged open. Ryan tore into the bedroom, naked apart from his boxer shorts.

"Ry," I said. "Did you hear what I—?"

"Jonno," Ryan gasped. "Coming up the path. Here. Any second."

Eve's eyes widened with horror. Letting go of my arm she rolled off the bed and onto the floor. She wriggled under the bed as I sat up, mouth gaping.

Two loud knocks echoed on the door.

"Oh my God," Eve whimpered from under the bed.

"Sssh," Ryan hissed. "*Shit*, you can see her. Pull the covers down."

I tugged at the sheet covering the bed, dragging it across so that it draped over the side, down to the floor.

Another loud thump on the door. "Lance! Are you in there?"

The sound of a key fumbling in the lock.

"Shit, shit, shit." Ryan tipped a heap of his dirty clothes beside the sheet.

Eve curled up in a little ball, now completely hidden.

The door opened. I looked round, knowing my face was on fire. Jonno stood in the doorway, his hands on his hips, staring suspiciously at me. He glanced across at Ryan, still standing beside my bed in his boxer shorts.

"Why didn't you answer?" he barked.

I gulped.

"I was about to get in the shower," Ryan said, nervously. "Er . . . sir."

Jonno looked back at me. "It's Lance I need to see."

I could almost feel the relief radiating off Ryan. He turned and practically ran into the bathroom.

I walked towards Jonno, hoping to keep his eyes away from my bed. He was looking round the room.

"Bloody mess in here," he snapped.

"I know," I said uneasily. "Sorry. We were gonna tidy up."

Jonno glared at me. Then his face split into a huge grin. "Yeah, right," he said. "Anyway, that's not why I'm here." He rubbed his hands together. "We have to talk."

I nodded. What the hell was coming now?

"My crèche manager tells me she found you with one of the girls. Is that right?"

I nodded again. *Oh crap.*

Jonno stared at me solemnly. "Do you remember my number one rule?"

"Yes sir. Don't embarrass the guests. Er . . . but I didn't . . . there weren't any. We were in the store room." I suddenly remembered Eve was listening. "Not that anything happened, sir," I added hastily. "It was all a misunderstanding."

"Stop, stop, stop." Jonno grinned at me. "I told you, I don't care who you shag on the staff. I know who the girl was. Between you and me I wouldn't mind some of that myself. No, what I'm talking about is you getting your end away on my time. *And* upsetting my crèche manager. Running that rug-rat hellhole's a nightmare job. I don't want her walking out on me."

"No, sir," I breathed. "It won't happen ag— I mean. . ."

"Relax." Jonno clapped his meaty hand down on my

shoulder. "What's done is done. But apart from apologising to Pilar, which I want you to do as soon as I've gone, I don't want you going near the crèche again. No more shift-swapping. Deal?" His eyes twinkled.

I looked at him, uncertain if he really meant everything was all right.

"And you do double shifts at the restaurant tomorrow to make up. Okay?"

I nodded.

"Good." Jonno strode over to the door. He turned, his fingers resting on the handle. "By the way, you haven't seen Eve, have you?"

I blinked. "No, sir."

He pursed his lips. "Well, if you do, tell her we're going out at eleven. See you later, Lance."

As the door slammed behind him I sank down onto Ryan's bed, my legs suddenly shaking.

Ryan peered out from the bathroom door, now fully dressed in his shorts and T-shirt. "Bloody hell, that was close," he said. "What was all that about the crèche store room?"

I glanced at Eve, who was scrambling out from under the sheet hanging over my bed.

"Tell you later." I glared at Ryan to shut up, then ran my hand through my hair. It was okay. Jonno hadn't seen

Eve. He wasn't even that cross about me messing up my shift.

I breathed out slowly. Relief flooded through me. We'd made it. I grinned, suddenly feeling exhilarated.

"Thank God he didn't see Eve," I said. "He'd have gone ballistic at me."

"At you?" Ryan raised his eyebrows. "I was the one standing here in my freakin' boxers."

We both started laughing.

I looked over at Eve. She was standing in front of the bed, hugging her arms round her chest. Her face was as white as the sheet she had hidden behind.

"What is it?" I stopped laughing and strode over to her. She was shivering. "Hey. Hey." I pulled her into a hug. "It's okay. He's gone. Nothing happened."

Eve backed away from me. "Nothing happened?" Her lip trembled. "What about what he said?"

I frowned. "Said? About what?" *Oh God.* "You mean about Catalina and the store room?"

"Catalina?" Ryan said.

I held out my hand, trying to shut him up. A tear was rolling down Eve's face. "Eve? What is it? I told you. Nothing happened."

She stared at me. "I don't mean that. It was my dad. Didn't you hear him? The way he was talking about

Catalina. She's my age. And he was all . . . ugh . . . it was disgusting. Like he fancied her himself. . ." Her voice cracked. "Like it was all boys together. *Shag who you like except if it's my daughter.*' He's such a hypocrite."

I shook my head, not knowing what on earth to say to her.

Ryan put his hand on her arm. "Hey, Eve. It's not such a biggie. Your dad just likes girls. You know?"

Eve threw him a disgusted glance, then looked back at me. "I'm not going out with him tonight. I'll do my songs. Then I'm going to tell him I'm not feeling well." Her mouth set in a determined line. "I'm going to come to the Garito and have fun with you and everyone."

I threw my arms around her and hugged her. *Yes.*

Over her shoulder Ryan was mouthing "Catalina?" at me.

"Go away," I mouthed back, jerking my thumb towards the door for added emphasis.

Ryan stood there for a second, staring at me. Then he picked up my iPod and left.

15

The row

It was eleven. The Garito was just starting to get going, the music pounding so hard it made the floorboards jump. Eve wasn't there yet. I'd already seen Catalina in the distance – looking murderously sexy in a black mini-dress – and was trying to avoid her.

I got plenty of looks and nudges from the other male staff. Gossip about what I'd done in the store room had been flying round the hotel all day, getting wildly exaggerated on the way. Chloe heard a version of the story in which Catalina and I had been caught without any clothes on, while Ryan heard a rumour that three other girls were involved too. I'd apologised to a very sniffy Pilar earlier, and had to promise never to go near the crèche for the rest of my stay.

"You're going to have to say something to Marco too,

you know," Ryan shouted in my ear. "Apparently he's off his head about it. God knows what he thinks you actually did."

"Why?" I groaned. "Why can't everyone just forget about it?"

Ryan rolled his eyes. "Don't be so lame. Anyway, he knows we're friends. If you don't explain, he's not going to want to hang out with me either."

I glared at him.

Ryan grinned. "I'll talk to him first, okay?"

Marco was sitting in a corner, hunched over a beer. I watched Ryan stroll over. At first Marco turned away, but Ryan sat down next to him anyway. He started talking and smiling and somehow, gradually, Marco shifted round and started talking too. Ryan looked up at me. I saw Marco follow his gaze. *Christ*. He was glowering at me like he wished I was dead.

I'd be lucky if he didn't try and punch me.

A few minutes later, Ryan sauntered back. "He's pretty mad at you," he said. "You're going to have to tell him about Eve. I don't think he'll believe it otherwise."

"But suppose he tells Jonno?"

Ryan let out an exasperated sigh. "You should have thought of that before you got into a bloody snogfest with Catalina, shouldn't you?"

Ryan, of course, had guessed exactly what had happened in the store room. I made a face at him and wandered over to Marco. He didn't look up.

"Can I talk to you?" I shouted over the music.

Marco nodded curtly. We went outside and wandered down to the trees. There was a strong wind blowing off the sea tonight. The palm tree branches swayed and creaked above our heads.

"Nothing happened," I said, my stomach churning. "Me and Catalina. Nothing. We were just looking for a mop."

Marco stared at me blankly.

"Cleaning things." I mimed mopping a floor. "There was a mess on the floor. Lots of paint. We had to clear it up."

I held my breath.

Marco squinted at me. He was quite a bit shorter than me. I had the strong feeling that he was weighing up his chances of beating me in a fight.

"Before. When I say I know lots of girls for you. I do not mean for you take *my* girl."

"I told you, I didn't. I—"

"Then why you at crèche?"

I took a deep breath, realising Ryan had been right. "I was there because I wanted to see Eve. You know. Eva. Ly-eeha-del-effy."

Marco stared at me. "*La hija del jefe?* Eva? Señor Ripley's Eva?"

I nodded.

Marco's eyes widened into circles. "*Eva?*" he said incredulously. "*Eres loco.* You mad. If Señor Ripley know this, he—"

"He doesn't know," I said. "But Eve is my girlfriend."

With perfect timing, Eve chose that minute to wander into view. I waved her over. She ran up, smiling at me. I put my arm round her. Instantly the smile fell and she pulled away.

"It's okay," I said. "I just told Marco about us. I *had* to," I said meaningfully. "He didn't understand why I was doing a crèche shift."

"Oh." Eve turned to Marco. "Please don't say anything, Marco," she pleaded. "My dad would be sooo mad."

I put my arm round her again and kissed her on the side of the head – just to make sure Marco had got the message.

He beamed. "Okay. I see now. I say nothing." He looked up at me. "I sorry for no believing you and Catalina."

"No worries," I said, feeling only slightly guilty. After all, nothing *had* happened with Cat. I had to keep reminding myself of that.

Marco went back into the Garito. Eve took my hand. "Don't you want to go in and dance?" she said.

133

"In a bit," I said. Apart from not wanting to be anywhere near Catalina, I was enjoying having Eve to myself for once. "Why don't we go for a walk, first."

Eve grinned at me. Exactly the same sexy grin I'd seen her give her boyfriend Ben, the first time I'd ever seen her.

"Mmmn," she said. "How far should we go?" She raised an eyebrow.

"Far as you want," I smiled, curving my arm round her shoulders.

We walked a long way down the beach. The sea hissed and spat at the shore, throwing up a salty breeze that gusted across our faces. Eve talked about her dad again. How much she loved him, but how little he understood her.

I listened as she raged and cried, wishing there was something I could do or say that would make her feel better.

At last she stopped and turned to me. "I'm sorry for going on and on," she said. "You've been so brilliant. And you've stopped being jealous and everything. And all I do is get upset about my dad."

I ran my hands down her back. She gave a tiny, sexy gasp.

"Maybe not *all* you do," I murmured.

An hour later we strolled back to the Garito, our arms wrapped round each other. We went inside and danced for a bit. Ryan and Chloe were both there too and even seeing

Catalina across the room couldn't spoil how I felt. This was what being on holiday should be about. Friends. Good music. Having fun. Being with Eve.

We left at one-thirty, so Eve could get back to her room before Jonno came back from his meal out. I walked with Eve up to the main lobby, then slipped away to the room Ryan and I shared. I fell asleep instantly and woke the next morning feeling that nothing could possibly spoil the rest of the holiday. . .

It was a hard day. A late-morning pool shift with Chloe, followed by my usual homework for Mum, then two exhausting shifts in a row in the restaurant. I staggered out at eight o'clock that evening and went back to the room to change. At quarter to nine I was out and heading towards the pool. I was, for once, actually looking forward to Open Mike Night. Ry and Chloe were planning on singing a duet – and because Lola only had to perform for the first half-hour, there would be no breaks, which meant Eve wouldn't have to sing herself. I was hoping that after we'd heard Ry and Chloe, the two of us could sneak off somewhere together.

As I got closer to the pool I could hear raised voices.

Was that Jonno? I had never heard him shouting. Eve told me he frequently lost his temper with the senior members of staff, but never in public.

I sped up, turned the corner past the trees and came face to face with Lola and Jonno having a massive argument by the pool.

I joined the crowd of hotel guests watching them from the pool bar. Lola was still in her jeans. For some reason the first thought that struck me was that she wasn't changed, even though she had to be on stage in less than fifteen minutes. What was she doing?

"For goodness sake, Jonno. How can you be so blind?" Lola's face was scarlet, her arms waving wildly through the air.

"Be quiet." Jonno's face was bright red as well. He was obviously making a huge effort not to shout again. Instead he kept reaching out, trying to pull Lola away. More hotel guests were arriving, clearly drawn by Lola's shrieks. The few remaining little kids still in the water, were being bundled away by anxious-looking mums and dads.

I spotted Eve, Chloe and Alejandro standing on the terrace by the lobby entrance and raced round to them.

"Get your hands off me," Lola screamed.

I reached the others. "What the hell's going on?" I said.

Eve shook her head. "Lola's gone mental."

"Totally off her head." Chloe glanced at me. "She was talking to Jonno at the bar and then, out of nowhere, boom."

136

"Like she exploded," Alejandro added.

"No waaaay." Lola's ear-splitting screech made me jump. "Don't you dare say that. I wasn't drunk. It *was* her."

A large crowd had now gathered behind Lola on the grass. Jonno glanced round, taking in all the people watching them. He moved even closer to Lola, talking rapidly. His face was grim: jaw clenched, eyes narrowed. He looked to me as if he'd like nothing better than to push Lola into the pool.

"Talk about embarrassing the guests," Chloe giggled.

"For Crissakes," Lola shouted. "Don't you even want to know who she was with?"

Jonno shook his head in frustration. I could see his mouth forming the words, "calm down".

"Don't tell me to calm down," Lola shrieked. "Just because you can't accept your daughter's more adult than you want her to be."

What?

Eve was wide-eyed beside me. "Why's she talking about me?"

"SHUT UP!" Jonno exploded.

There was a shocked silence round the pool. Lola stared at him triumphantly. "I saw her last night," she said. Her voice was quieter now, but the pool area was so still she would have been heard if she'd whispered. "I saw her going into a boy's room at two-thirty last night." Lola pointed to where we were all standing on the grass near the hotel terrace. "She was with him."

Now everyone was looking at us.

I blinked rapidly. Lola *must* have been drunk. I hadn't been with Eve that late. I'd left her at the hotel at, what, one-thirty? Certainly not after two. And she hadn't been in my room at all yesterday evening.

And then I realised Lola wasn't pointing at me. I looked down the line of us – from Eve, to Chloe to Alejandro.

I stared at Alejandro. The tan had turned to a deathly grey. There was fear written all over his face. And something else. Something unmistakable. Guilt.

No. It couldn't be true. It must have been some other girl. Eve would say so. I gripped her arm. "Eve?" I said, hoarsely. "What's she talking about?"

But Eve was pulling away from me, moving towards Alejandro. Jonno was pounding over, breathing heavily. Seconds later he was beside them, fists clenched at his side. He looked at Eve.

"Is this true? Did you go to his room last night?"

The whole world shrank to Eve's face.

She stood in front of Alejandro, her arms spread out, protecting him from her father.

"Yes," she said.

16

The truth about Alejandro

I know Eve carried on talking, but I didn't hear what she said. I couldn't breathe. I just stood there, feeling like I'd been punched in the stomach.

It couldn't be true. She was with me. We were perfect. Together. Why would she go after someone else?

I thought of Catalina. How easy that would have been. My heart sank.

The pianist from the band was tugging at Jonno's arm.

"Is nine o'clock, Señor Ripley," he moaned. "We have no singer. No drummer."

Jonno loomed over Alejandro, his nostrils flaring, his whole face clenched with rage.

"I'll deal with you after the Open Mike." He grabbed Alejandro's arm and dragged him into the main lobby and towards the stairs down to the nightclub.

In the distance I could now hear the pianist and Lola shrieking at each other. But my eyes were fixed on Eve.

"Eve?" I said, hoarsely. "Please. What's happening?"

I still couldn't believe that she had been with Alejandro last night. She turned to me distractedly.

"Luke, it's not how it looks."

"What *happened*?"

Eve glanced into the hotel. "I did go to his room. He called me. But nothing happened, I promise. He doesn't even fancy me."

"You're telling me—?"

"I have to go and make sure Alejandro's all right." Eve edged towards the hotel door. Her eyes were full of tears. "Please, just trust me on this. Nothing happened."

She turned and fled into the hotel.

I stared after her. There was this empty hole where my insides should have been, like someone had ripped them all out. I felt Chloe's hand on my arm.

"Luke?" she said gently.

"Did you know?" I realised my hands were shaking and balled them into fists.

"I knew they were close, but . . . look, if Eve says nothing happened you should believe her."

I gazed at her, numbly. "She went to his room in the middle of the night, Chlo."

As I said the words the knowledge that it was true – and of what that must mean – finally sank in. The shock I'd felt lifted. Rage boiled up from my stomach. I tore my arm away from Chloe's hand and strode indoors.

Dimly, in the background, I could hear her calling after me. I saw Ryan in the main lobby.

"What's going on?" he said, seeing my face. "Luke?"

I raced past him and down the steps to the nightclub.

Jonno was already on the stage. He was standing further back than usual, next to the drum kit.

"Ladies and Gentlemen. Welcome to Open Mike Night at La Villa Bonita."

I could see Alejandro behind the drums. He hadn't noticed me. Jealousy twisted its knife into my gut. He had smiled and smiled at me and all the time he was after Eve.

With a jolt I remembered that first evening we'd gone out for a drink in Cala del Toro. How Alejandro had walked Eve back to the hotel. Is that when it had started? Or later, after his dad arrived and they went out for all those late night meals together?

I looked around for Eve. She wasn't sitting at our usual table. No-one was. I scanned the room. There. She was at the far edge of the stage, looking anxiously up at Alejandro. At *him*. . .

The knife twisted deeper. How dare she? I'd given her my heart and she'd thrown it away like garbage.

Blood pumped through my head. I could hardly breathe. I stormed towards the stage.

Eve caught sight of me as I started pushing past tables full of people.

She shook her head then, seeing I was still coming, rushed forwards to meet me.

Jonno had finished making his announcements now. He was talking to one of the waiters, one eye still fixed on Alejandro. There was no sign of Lola. Jonno had obviously decided to go straight into the open mike session. The first singer was on stage, warbling out of tune.

Eve and I reached each other at Jonno's regular – and still empty – table, just under the stage. She slid into the nearest chair, motioning me into the next seat.

I gritted my teeth and sat down. It was taking every bit of self-restraint I had not to yell at her. But I didn't want to start yelling yet. I needed to hear her say it first. Admit what she'd done.

"Please don't make a big fuss, Luke," she said quietly. "Alejandro and I were just talking."

I clenched my hands more tightly. The knife in my gut twisted again.

"Don't lie to me," I said. "People don't go to each other's rooms at two in the morning to talk."

"We *were*," Eve insisted. "Why won't you-—?"

"What were you talking about?" I spat. "How you like being kissed? Or maybe how he likes it? Because he's so fit you'd do anything to please him, wouldn't you?"

Eve stared at me as if she was seeing me for the first time.

The first open mike singer finished to a polite smattering of applause.

"If I say nothing happened, that means nothing happened. Why won't you—?"

"Because it's rubbish. I know you fancy him. You always fancied him—"

"I don't. I didn't."

"So what, then? What did you talk about?"

I stopped, my breath jerky and shallow.

"We were talking about . . . stuff. About someone he needs to speak to. Look, I can't tell you. I can't tell anyone. I promised him."

The knife sliced up through my heart. "You promised *him*?" I hissed. "You promised *him*? What about me? What about us? You *bitch*."

Eve blinked at me. Tears welled up in her eyes. "Fine."

"What d'you mean 'fine'?" I stared at her. "Are you dumping me?"

She pressed her lips together and looked down at the tablecloth.

My breath caught in my throat. "Are you going out with him?"

Eve said nothing.

I stood up and caught sight of Ryan and Chloe staring at us, horrorstruck, from the other end of the table.

Unable to meet their gaze I turned and stumbled, blindly, out of the room.

The next two hours were the worst I'd ever lived. I went down to the beach and found a deserted spot in the trees about three or four hundred yards along. I curled up in the leaf-strewn sandy grass and lay there, flooded with waves of rage and jealousy and humiliation. For the first time since we'd arrived at La Villa Bonita, it rained. A soft spattering rain that trickled down the leaves on the trees above and dripped onto me.

After a while I heard Ryan walking along the beach, calling out my name. I didn't answer. There was nothing to say. *I* was nothing. Without Eve I was no-one.

I loved her so much and she didn't love me at all.

Misery swamped me, tears and rain running down my cheeks. And then the fear – the terrible emptiness of being without her. She couldn't leave me. I couldn't let her go. She couldn't want him instead.

Him.

The storm of feelings in my head settled into a single focus.

Alejandro. That smooth *bastard*.

I got up and went back to the hotel. It was almost eleven o'clock. I knew the Open Mike Night would be drawing to a close and that the confrontation between Jonno and Alejandro was about to happen.

I wanted to be there.

I had completely forgotten how unreasonable I used to think Jonno was about Eve. I wanted to see Alejandro suffer.

I wanted to inflict some suffering of my own.

The nightclub was emptying when I arrived. I saw Jonno instantly. He was still firmly planted next to Alejandro and the drum kit, chatting with some of the guests.

Chloe rushed up to me. "Luke, where've you been? Oh, God, you're all wet. Ry and I were looking everywhere for you."

I looked past her, searching the room for Eve. There she was. Still standing near the stage, looking anxiously across at her father and Alejandro.

The guests were drifting out now. There would be a ten-minute break while the DJ set up for the rubbish disco that came on every night. I could see Jonno checking how many people were left.

145

"Luke, man." Ryan's voice was gentle. Sympathetic. "Why don't we go outside. Get a beer. Just go somewhere and chill."

I shook my head, still staring at the stage. "I want to be here."

Ryan and Chloe exchanged alarmed glances. "I don't think that's a good idea." Ryan touched my arm. "Come on, let's go."

I shook his hand off angrily. "Leave me alone." I strode towards the stage. The other musicians had gone now. Jonno was giving his last cheery handshake to a guest, his last instruction to a waiter. Then he was free. I could see the fury in his face as he turned and gripped Alejandro by the arm.

They were speaking. I couldn't hear what they were saying. I moved nearer. Eve was fluttering nervously next to them both. Jonno was clearly telling her to go. She was equally obviously refusing.

Jonno looked round, taking in the number of guests still sitting around, chatting. He turned and strode backstage, his beefy hand still gripping Alejandro's arm. Eve fol-lowed.

I leaped up onto the stage after her, sensing Ryan and Chloe behind me.

I had been backstage many times since Eve started

singing every night. It was always dark, a warren of corridors, doors, painted screens propped against walls, lighting rigs above your head. I followed the glittery swish of Eve's dress along the corridor, past the dressing rooms and out the back.

A little alleyway, bricked off from the rest of the hotel. Nothing but dustbins. My heart started beating faster. Jonno had Alejandro pinned against the brick wall. Alejandro was struggling, but although he was tall and broad-shouldered, Jonno was simply bigger and stronger.

Rain poured down. Jonno's hair was already plastered to his head.

"You evil little shit. If you weren't my partner's son you'd be dead."

"Eve and me is talking," Alejandro said, his masterful English deserting him. "Talking. There was nothing bad."

"Daddy, stop." Eve tugged at Jonno's arm. He didn't appear to notice her.

"Talking?" Jonno shouted. "I know what kind of talking goes on in the middle of the night. Talking innocent girls into bed talking."

In the midst of my pleasure at seeing Alejandro literally backed up against a wall, I felt a pinprick of irritation at Jonno's inability to see Eve as she was.

Innocent, my arse.

She was about as innocent as a rattlesnake.

"Daddy, listen. Alejandro was upset. He had to talk to me about something important. Please." I could hear the tears in Eve's voice. Her face was wet, shining in the rain.

"It is true, Señor Ripley." Alejandro choked as Jonno's hand tightened round his neck.

"Oh God," Chloe breathed. I looked round. She and Ryan were standing next to me by the door, open-mouthed.

"He was upset, Daddy. He just needed a friend," Eve pleaded, now trying to push her way between her father and Alejandro.

My heart twisted as I watched her. She wasn't even aware I was here. All she cared about was saving that bastard's skin.

"Daddy, listen."

Jonno suddenly straightened up, away from Alejandro, and turned on her. "SHUT UP, EVE," he roared. "You have no idea what you're talking about. If he was upset it was to . . . to get you into bed. If he said he needed a friend it was to turn you into something else."

I could feel myself nodding.

"I knew I should have insisted you went to a Catholic school," Jonno shouted. "That's one thing the Spanish get right."

"But nothing happened," Eve insisted, tears streaming down her face. "He didn't touch me. We were just talking."

"IT WAS THE MIDDLE OF THE NIGHT," Jonno bellowed.

"Don't say, Eva," Alejandro pleaded.

She looked at him, shaking her head.

Jonno shoved Alejandro against the wall again.

In that second I flashbacked to the night Ben beat me up. The same terror I'd felt was in Alejandro's eyes now. For a moment the old panic rose in me. I pushed it away as Jonno drew back his fist. *Yes.* Hate burned like acid in my chest.

"What could possibly explain my daughter being in your room and you not taking advantage of her?" Jonno spat.

Alejandro stared back at him – silent and defiant.

"For God's sake, Dad," Eve sobbed. "He's not even into girls. He's gay."

17

A bunch of flowers

Time seemed to stop for a few seconds. I was suddenly aware of the rain falling on the roof behind me. A relentless spatter. Somewhere nearby an overflow pipe was gushing water into a drain. The world smelled damp and fresh.

Alejandro was gay? Which meant he wasn't into girls? Which meant he *wasn't* after Eve?

I stared at him. He was hanging his head, his face suddenly flushed. Then he looked up at Eve. He didn't say anything but the expression in his eyes was clear, even from where I was standing.

You've betrayed me.

"I'm sorry," Eve stammered.

"Gay?" Jonno let go of Alejandro's shoulder. He stood back, his forehead wrinkled in a frown. "Really?"

Alejandro said nothing.

Jonno's frown deepened. "Does your dad know?"

"No." Alejandro glared at him. "I do not choose to tell him yet." He looked away and caught sight of me and Chloe and Ryan over by the door. His face flooded a deeper red, then he muttered something in Spanish and turned and strode away round the side of the alley.

My heart was beating fast. I was so used to thinking that every guy who saw Eve wanted her that I was finding it difficult to absorb what had just happened and what it meant.

Jonno looked equally confused. He made no attempt to follow Alejandro. Instead, he brushed his wet hair from his face and turned to Eve. "What were you doing in his room so late?"

Eve put her hands on her hips. "I told you," she said. "We were talking. He'd just got back from your meal and he was really upset about his dad. He's desperate to come out to his family, but he's terrified of what they'll say. They're very traditional, Dad. You *know* that."

Jonno nodded slowly. "He's totally gay? He's sure?"

"Yes." Eve gripped his arm. "You won't say anything to his dad, will you?"

I watched them, a delicious glow spreading through my entire body. Eve wasn't after Alejandro. He wasn't after her. They were friends, like she'd said. Just talking. Which meant she must still want me.

151

"Eve." I took a step towards her, my whole face stretched in a smile.

Eve and Jonno spun round. Eve's mouth fell open.

"What are you doing here?" Jonno roared.

"I just want to talk to Eve." I was still grinning at her. If I could just get her on her own, everything would be all right.

"Get out of it," Jonno bellowed.

Ryan grabbed my arm. "Not now." He dragged me backwards towards the stage door.

I struggled against him. Eve had turned back to her dad. Jonno had his arm round her shoulders, guiding her past the wall and out of the alley. "I have to talk to her."

"Later, man." Ryan pulled me through the stage door. Chloe slammed it shut behind us and leaned against it, blocking my way out.

The thud of the disco bass echoed in the distance.

"No." I pulled away from Ryan.

He yanked me back again. "The last thing Eve needs is to have to stop her dad beating up on *another* guy."

"Ryan's right." I felt Chloe's hand on my arm. "Let it go for now. You'll see her in the morning."

I slumped back against the wall. It didn't matter. Like Chloe said, I would see Eve in the morning. Everything was sorted now. I was suddenly aware of my damp shirt clinging to my back. Soaked to the skin, and exhausted. Completely drained, like I could hardly stand up.

"Okay." I straightened up and reached for the door leading outside again. "I'm going to bed." Chloe stood back as I opened the door and dragged myself back out, into the soft, falling rain.

I slept late the next morning. When I woke the sun was streaming in through the open window. I could hear the faint squeals of excitement from the kids in the pool, and birds singing in the trees round the back of the room. I leaped out of bed, determined to find Eve straight away.

Ryan had left me a text:

E & C in crèche til 12. c u l8r. R.

Crap. It was now ten-thirty. I didn't dare go anywhere near the crèche. Never mind. I would go and get a headstart on Mum's homework. Then meet Eve when she finished. I checked the timetable for the week. Good. My waiting tables shift didn't begin until four this afternoon. Even allowing for homework time and Eve's rehearsal, we should get an hour or two together.

I showered, pulled on some long shorts and a T-shirt and raced happily up to the stuffy little office. I'd started leaving my homework papers in there. Jonno didn't seem to mind, and it saved lugging them backwards and forwards from the room. I rifled through the English language work-sheets, pulling out what I knew I was supposed to be working on today. Then I switched on the computer and checked my emails. There was one from Mum.

Dear Luke, Here's another scan of the baby. This one a bit clearer I think. I'm still sure it's a boy. You have been so good with your homework I've decided to let you off the last ten days. You deserve a break. All my love, Mum.

I stared at the email, reading it twice to make sure I'd properly understood.

Yeees.

No more stupid homework. I'd have masses more time with Eve now. I quickly opened up the attachment. Another grainy, black and white photograph. I squinted at it. How was that any clearer? Never mind, I'd look at it later. Chloe had loved the last scan. I clicked on the printer icon and waited impatiently for the picture to appear.

I sent Mum an email.

Thanks, you are brilliant. Is baby really there – can't work out where any of it is! lots of love. L.

I grinned. Just the sort of email Mum would like.

I pressed send, scrunched the scan up in my pocket and shoved all my old homework sheets in the bin. Seconds later I was switching off the computer and heading out the door, happier than I could ever remember feeling.

I wandered down to the pool, where Marco was on duty. We chatted for a bit. Apparently Lola had walked out after her row with Jonno last night. No-one had seen her since.

"She go," Marco said dramatically. "And she take her big chest also." He grinned at me. "I shall miss."

The news filled me with further happiness. Eve hated Lola. If Lola had left, Eve would be ecstatic. The day was getting better and better.

I wandered down to the crèche just before twelve. I could see Pilar outside in the playground. Chloe was there too, grimly pushing three little girls on the swings. She looked bored as hell.

No sign of Eve. She must be indoors.

Not wanting to risk Pilar's wrath by getting too close, I sat a hundred yards or so away in the shade of the olive trees. The grass was still a little damp from last night, but the sun was burning hot now in a bright blue sky. It was a beautiful day. A perfect day. While I was waiting I picked a few wild flowers from under the trees. Eve always loved little romantic gestures like that. It wasn't often I thought of them. But I did today.

Then I sat and waited.

She came out at five past twelve, looking round for Chloe. The two of them sauntered along the path together, waving goodbye to Pilar. The sun glinted off Eve's blonde hair as she walked. She was wearing jeans and her Bonita Babe T-shirt was filthy with paint and glue. I didn't think she'd ever looked more beautiful. I rushed over, the little bunch of flowers gripped tightly in my hand.

Eve and Chloe were deep in conversation and didn't see me until I was right in front of them. Eve looked up. She didn't smile.

"Eve?" I said.

I was grinning, so sure she would be happy to see me. But she looked away.

I stepped closer. "Eve?" I touched her arm.

She whipped it away like I'd burned her. "I don't want to talk to you."

What? I glanced at Chloe, bewildered. Chloe bit her lip. I motioned her to go away. With a look at Eve, Chloe sighed and slunk off.

I moved round in front of Eve. The sun was fierce on the back of my neck. "Eve? What's wrong?"

She looked up at me, her eyes full of contempt. "You didn't believe me."

"You mean about Alejandro?" I frowned. "But . . . but I didn't understand before. He's . . . it's like you were with a girlfriend or something. I get it, now."

Eve's eyes were like chips of ice. "You don't get it at all, Luke. I asked you to trust me and you didn't."

"But you admitted you were in his room." I clenched my fists, every nerve and muscle in my body tensed with the effort of making her see that I hadn't been unreasonable.

"You acted just like my dad. Worse. At least he was only angry at Alejandro. *You* thought I was two-timing you."

"But you've got to see how it looked to me."

"No, Luke," she said. "How about *you* trying to see how not trusting me looked to *me*?"

I stared at her, panic whirling in my chest.

And then she said it.

"I can't go out with you any more."

She took a step past me.

No. No. No. This isn't happening.

I spun round. Grabbed her arm. "You can't dump me for being jealous," I said. "It's because I want you so much. Because I love you."

"You don't love me." Eve snatched her arm away. "I thought you did, but I can see now you don't understand what the word means."

"I do." Panic filled my head. I had to make her see.

"No you don't." Eve's breathing was harsh. Uneven. "You don't have a clue."

"Listen." I reached out for her again.

Eve pulled away. "Leave me alone. You don't know what

you're talking about. You don't know anything about being in a relationship."

I blinked at her, too shocked to speak. How could she think that?

"You're pathetic," she snarled. "You're so immature you're pathetic."

No. That wasn't fair. My temper rose.

"*I'm* not the immature one." I glared at her. "*You're* the one who goes all little girly round your dad. No wonder he acts like he does. He probably thinks you're still six."

Eve tossed her head and stalked away from me. I strode after her.

"And you're scared," I shouted, insight flashing like lightning through the thunder in my mind. "You're terrified that if he sees you as a grown-up then he won't love you any more."

Eve turned on me, her face scarlet.

"THAT'S NOT TRUE!" she yelled.

A couple of hotel guests strolling past stared at her.

Eve didn't even see them. She moved closer. So close I could feel the heat coming off her face.

"That *so* isn't true, Luke, but I'll tell you something that is." She gritted her teeth. "I did fancy Alejandro. And if he hadn't been gay I would have snogged his face off."

And with that she spun round and marched off down the path.

I stood, rooted to the spot. The sun was in my eyes as I watched her reach the pool. Everything was bleached out, a glaring white. My mind was numb. Totally numb.

I caught sight of the little bunch of flowers in my fist. The heads were starting to wilt in the harsh midday sun.

I opened my hands and let them fall to the ground.

18

Alone

The next few days passed in a slow, burning blur of misery. I felt best when I was angry, full of hate against Eve and Alejandro and everyone. But too often the anger dissolved and the bottom fell out of my world as I ached to be with Eve and knew that she didn't want me.

Lola had walked out on Jonno and her job with the band. Still, he seemed to be coping with being dumped better than I was. He hired two new singers and was rumoured to be dating the hotel's chief receptionist – a twenty-something blonde with great legs – the very next day.

Chloe and Eve got their GCSE results. Chloe had done really well – loads of As and Bs, despite having hardly worked for most of the year. She said Eve had passed everything, though not with such good grades overall. Still, she'd got an A* for Art and I knew that that was all Eve really cared about.

Chloe also told me that Eve had finally put her foot down about singing with the band, so she no longer had to rehearse in the afternoons and spend half her evenings in the nightclub. It was ironic. After weeks of hardly being able to see each other, we both, suddenly, had masses of spare time. Not that Eve started coming to the Garito or anywhere she thought I might hang out. But she took to sunbathing a lot by the pool. I often saw her there – usually being chatted up by one of the hotel guests – but I never went up to her.

I couldn't get what she'd said about Alejandro out of my head. Jealousy ate away at me. I swung between violent fury at them both and this dark, deep, empty misery, where I imagined falling at her knees and begging her to take me back.

After two days of watching me mooch unhappily around the hotel Ryan insisted I came with him and Chloe to the Garito that night. I'd been avoiding it, going back to the room early instead. I couldn't bear the thought of being with people having fun.

"You can't stay here by yourself again," Ryan said, buttoning up his shirt. He chucked me a top from my pile of clothes on the floor. "Here. Put this on."

I stared at the top. It was one Eve had made me buy back in London. It was dark blue. She'd said it brought out the colour of my eyes.

I smiled to myself. She was always coming out with arty rubbish like that. But then I remembered how she'd looked at me when she'd held the top up against my face. How her eyes had shone as she'd said I'd look really, really hot in it.

"Look, man," Ryan said. "There's a million other girls out there. Half the staff here think you're some kind of sex god. *El Rubio*, remember? I bet we go down there and you're fighting off some horny Spanish babe within ten minutes."

I picked up the dark blue top. "I don't think so, and anyway—"

"It'll do you good." Ryan grinned. "Unless you'd rather carry on sulking."

"I'm not sulking," I snapped.

Ryan pointed at the top. "Prove it," he said.

We arrived at the Garito just before midnight. The music was blaring out as usual. Chloe stopped in the doorway to pull on her heels. As she bent over, brushing the sand from her feet, Ryan nudged me in the ribs.

"Check out what Cat's wearing," he said.

I peered round the gloomy room. It was heaving with

people, most of them dancing. I caught sight of Catalina chatting with a group of girls on the far side of the music deck. She had on this tiny top and then – *Jesus* – what looked like a strip of rough leather wound round her curvy hips. It couldn't have been more than a few centimetres long, beginning below where her hipbones jutted out and ending at the very tops of her slender legs.

"Whoa," I said, completely unable to look away.

Beside me, Chloe snorted. "I've seen bigger belts," she said. "Oh, for God's sake, Luke, stop drooling."

"Yeah, come on, man." Ryan punched my arm. "Cat's with Marco. Have a look round. See what else you fancy."

I wandered after them towards Marco and a group of hotel workers we often shared pool and restaurant shifts with. Ryan and Chloe started chatting away. A couple of girls caught my eye and smiled at me, but I found myself looking round for Catalina. She'd vanished behind a row of shaggy-haired males lined up next to the music deck.

After a while Ryan and Chloe dragged me onto the dance floor. The music was awesome. Loud and pounding. Really sexy and bass-heavy. But my heart just wasn't in it. I could see Catalina and Marco dancing together on the other side of the room. Everyone else was swaying together, completely caught up in the music. I felt lonelier than I had done when I'd been on my own.

I backed away a little, then turned and slipped outside. I wandered down to the trees and stared out at the glistening sea. A few peaceful minutes passed, the only sound the thump of the music behind me and the shush of the waves and the trees.

Then I felt a small hand on my arm.

"Hi, *Rubio*." Catalina was grinning up at me.

"Hi." I looked down at the flat brown skin of her waist and how it hollowed out and disappeared under that ridiculously tiny skirt.

"You look great," I said, my earlier lust powering back.

Catalina slid her hand under my shirt and up my back. My skin erupted in goosebumps under her fingers.

"Mmmn," she said. "I thought maybe you no liking me?"

She clawed her hand lower. Over my jeans.

We stared at each other. I was suddenly so turned on I could hardly stand up. I reached out and pulled her towards me.

"Course I like you," I breathed.

Her mouth was wetter than Eve's. Her tongue darted against mine like a lizard, quick and fiery. Our snogging got deeper and harder. She was going to let me go further. I brought my hand round. Then, abruptly, she pulled back.

Totally sexed-up I reached out for her again. She shook her head.

"What?" My voice was all croaky.

She narrowed her eyes and smiled up at me. "You good kisser. But I want to dance too. Come with me?" She took my hand.

I nodded. Whatever. Wherever. Without thinking about anything other than how much I wanted her I followed her into the Garito.

The music was still blaring. The place was so crowded I had to let go of her hand as we pushed our way through the sweaty, heaving mass of dancing bodies. I kept my eyes fixed on her hard, curvy body, not noticing anything else. At last she stopped and turned round. She wriggled forwards and pressed up against me again, rolling her hips in time with the music.

I reached round her slim back and ran my hands down her narrow waist. Lower, lower until I felt the rough leather under my fingers. *Oh God.* I pulled her even closer, leaning down to find her mouth.

She kissed me back, her fingers sliding through my hair.

Then a hand gripped my shoulder, tugging at my shirt, pulling me backwards.

"Hey." I looked behind me.

It was Ryan. He glared at me and yanked harder on my

shirt. I stumbled backwards, losing hold of Catalina. The room was so crowded other people were already pushing between us.

I tried to shove Ryan away, but he wouldn't let go.

"What is it?" I yelled over the music. What was his problem? You never interrupt someone in the middle of a snog. That's just basic manners. Not unless the place is on fire or something.

"Out," he shouted, dragging me towards the door. "Come on."

I tried to wrench myself away but he still wouldn't let go. Swearing my head off, I gave up and let him haul me over to the door.

We jumped down into the sand.

"What's going on, Ry?"

Ryan clenched his jaw. "Have you got a death wish or something?" He prodded me back towards the trees.

"What the hell are you talking about?" I dug my heels into the sand and pushed him back. "What *is* it?"

Ryan shoved me in the chest with the flats of both hands. I stumbled backwards. I'd never seen him look so angry.

"Oh, don't bother to say thank you but I've just saved you from getting beaten up by Marco and his three enormous mates."

Marco.

My mouth fell open. I'd completely forgotten about him and Catalina.

"For some reason," Ryan went on, sarcastically, "Spanish boys don't like arseholes getting off with their girlfriends in front of them any more than English ones do."

I groaned. "Was Marco really mad?"

Ryan rolled his eyes. "Well, how would you feel if your incredibly hot girlfriend practically started having sex with someone else right under your nose?" He frowned. "Actually, Marco was more upset than anything. His friends were all up for kicking your head in, but Marco was almost in tears. God, Luke, it's one thing in a bloody store room. I mean, at least no-one else was there then. But in front of everyone . . . how could you humiliate him like that?"

"It was Cat," I said, weakly. "She came up to me out here. She was all . . . all into it. . ."

"For goodness sake." Ryan kicked at the sand.

"Then she dragged me inside." I hung my head, imagining how Marco must've felt when he'd seen us.

Ryan looked up. "I know she's a complete bitch but . . . *Jesus,* Luke . . . you did it too."

"I know."

We wandered down to the line of trees. A strong breeze

167

streamed in off the ocean, rustling the branches above our heads

"I didn't even think about Marco," I said.

"I bet Cat did – I bet she planned the whole thing. I bet she wanted Marco to see."

"Why?" I said. "Why would she do that?"

"I dunno. Maybe she likes blokes fighting over her."

I shivered, remembering the last fight I'd been in – how Ben and his friends had held me down and kicked and punched me. That fight had been over a girl, too. Over Eve. With a jolt I realised I'd done the same thing again. I'd gone after someone else's girl. More . . . I'd done exactly the thing I was so worried other guys would do with Eve.

But I didn't want to think about Eve.

"Wouldn't have been much of a fight," I said, attempting a grin. "Four against one."

Ryan bristled. "So you don't think I'd have jumped in and pulled you out?"

I stared at him. "I didn't mean it like that. God, Ryan, why are you so upset? It's not like she's *your* girlfriend."

He leaned against a tree. "I just feel sorry for Marco," he said quietly. He glanced at me. "What you did happened to me once. That older girl I told you about ages ago – my sister's friend. We'd been going out for a couple of months. Then one day we went to this club and I turned round and she was with this other guy. All over him. It was the worst moment of my life. Not just seeing her with someone else. But everyone else seeing too. Laughing at me. Feeling sorry for me. . ."

He looked at me, as if expecting me to say something.

"Jeez," I said. "Bummer."

Ryan pushed himself away from his tree and laughed. "You know, Chloe's right about you," he said. "She says you have the emotional intelligence of a woolly hat. No wonder Eve got pissed off."

My temper rose. This was too close to the truth.

"I'm going back to the room," I snapped.

"Good idea." Ryan turned away. He took a couple of steps then glanced at me over his shoulder. "Hey, Luke."

I raised my eyebrows. "What?"

Ryan shot me an exasperated grin. "Try not to get off with anyone else's girlfriend on your way." He headed back to the Garito.

I made a rude sign at his departing back.

Without turning round, he stuck his finger up at me.

I wandered along the beach. It was a beautiful night. Starry sky. Fresh sea smell. Strong, warm breeze. I wondered where Eve was.

Had she felt about Alejandro like I'd felt about Catalina? I

169

hated the thought of her wanting him, but in my heart I knew it wasn't really fair to be angry. I mean, I hadn't had a choice about finding Cat horny. At least it hadn't felt like I had.

What did it matter?

I fancied Cat like mad. What we'd just done together was still filling my head. But I knew I would happily never see her again in exchange for a single chance to get Eve to go back out with me. But Eve didn't want me. She wanted Alejandro.

An image of them together flashed into my mind. I gritted my teeth, trying to push it away.

I strolled through the trees and past the crèche. I glanced at the pool. For once it was empty. I didn't feel at all sleepy. And I badly needed to do something, anything, to take my mind off Eve and Alejandro.

I went over and dangled my hand over the side. The water felt warm. I looked round. No-one was here. I slipped off all my clothes and slid into the pool. Mmmm. I plunged under, pulling myself through the water with big, energetic strokes. It was ace having the place to myself. Usually you couldn't swim for more than a couple of metres without bumping into some screaming kid.

I stood, up to my waist in water, shaking the drops out of my hair. A pair of expensive-looking leather sandals planted themselves at the edge of the water. I looked up. And came face to face with the very last person I wanted to see.

19

Boy-on-boy chat-up procedures

Alejandro smiled down at me. His eyes flickered over my bare chest and I had two thoughts in quick succession.

One: this guy had cost me my girlfriend. One way or another it was all his fault and I wanted nothing more than to get out of the pool, right now, and punch him.

Two: he was gay and I was naked.

Thought two swamped thought one, obliterating any idea of my getting out of the pool. I crouched down in the water, hoping the floodlights were too far away to show any more of me than a vague pink blur.

"*Hola.*" Alejandro squatted down at the edge of the pool. "Are you okay?"

I nodded, glancing round to see how far away I was

from my clothes. Damn. They were at the other end of the pool.

"No towel?" Alejandro's eyes twinkled.

I stared at him blankly. *Was he flirting with me?*

Alejandro started unbuttoning his shirt. "Here. You can put this round you while you get out."

Jesus Christ. Another minute and we'd both be naked.

"No worries." I turned my back and waded, still in a crouching position, towards the deep end. "I'll get my clothes."

I splashed clumsily through the water. Somehow I had to get out of the pool and into my clothes without Alejandro seeing me. I looked over my shoulder. He was walking towards me again, his shirt still half unbuttoned.

Why wouldn't he just go away?

"Do you want to go for a drive with me?" he said.

I stopped and stared at him. He had to be kidding.

"No," I snapped. "All I want is to get out and get dressed. D'you mind?"

Alejandro's mouth curled into a massive grin. "It is no a date, Luke. I just want to talk to you."

I shrugged, gripping the side of the pool.

Go away.

Alejandro turned his back. "Okay," he said. "Get out. I

promise I won't look." He wandered away from me, back towards the shallow end.

This was clearly the best offer I was going to get. Keeping my eyes on him, I hauled myself out of the pool and tried to shove my dripping legs back into my jeans.

"Tell me, Luke," Alejandro said, his back still turned. "Do you like . . . want . . . every girl you see?"

I frowned, trying to push my foot through a kink of denim. "No," I said, suspiciously.

"And when you do see a girl you like, do you . . . how do you say . . . jump her bones . . . you know . . . without first seeing if she is interested?"

"No, of course not," I said, now busy with the other foot. At last I had both legs through my jeans.

Alejandro shook his head. "So why do you think I will with you?"

Jesus. On my current list of things I least wanted to do, talking about boy-on-boy chat-up procedures with a gay guy was pretty near the top.

I tugged my jeans up over my hips and pulled on the zip.

"Okay, fine." I picked up my top. "Anyway. I'm off. Bye."

Alejandro turned round. He spread his arms, his face an expressive mix of exasperation and amusement. "Hey, come on. Why are you so frightened? I am no trying to kiss you. Come for a drive. I want to tell you about Eva."

I glared at him, suddenly remembering the very first thought I'd had when I'd seen him at the side of the pool.

"I don't want to go anywhere with you."

I marched off, pulling my top over my head.

"Eva told me she said to you how much she liked me," Alejandro said. "She also told me she was lying. She wanted to hurt you. She told me."

I stopped, my heart thudding.

Alejandro walked up beside me. "Eva said things," he said quietly. "Things you should know. Please. Come for a drive. I have a cool car."

The car *was* cool. An Alpha Romeo Spider, all open and sleek, with a two-litre JTS engine. Alejandro revved us noisily out of the hotel drive and we sped off along the dark road. The moon hung low over the sea, catching the sparkle of distant waves. The wind was cold in my wet hair. I closed my eyes, letting the force of it press against my eyelids and cheeks and forehead.

Neither of us spoke. Alejandro played a rock track that I happened to really like. It roared into the peaceful landscape around us. After about fifteen minutes driving uphill Alejandro swung the car off the road onto a stony layby surrounded by bushes, overlooking the sea.

We got out of the car, and strolled to the cliff edge. The

silence hissed in my ears after the noise of the music. It was colder this high up. I shivered.

Alejandro stared out to sea. He sighed.

"I came here with my girlfriends, once."

"Girlfriends?"

He nodded. "Being gay. It's no like one day you suddenly know. In my heart I always like boys. Always. But since I was younger, you know, thirteen, fourteen, I try to like girls. And girls like me. It is easy. The kissing. The touching."

I raised my eyes. "Lucky you," I said.

Alejandro shook his head. "Not really. I mean it's okay with girls but in my heart I am lying. I am miserable. I look at boys. I imagine with boys. Later I have secret boyfriends. No-one knows. I feel guilty. And also *verguenza*. That is . . . how do you say it? . . . shame? Because I know this is the twenty-first century, but my parents are old. They have only daughters and me. They want me to be a proper man. Grow up. Marry a girl. All that. And I am lying to them. To myself. You understand?"

I nodded, though when I thought about it I wasn't at all sure that I did understand. I'd never considered what it must be like to feel so . . . so different from everyone else. What it must be like to worry so much about what other people thought of you.

"Then I meet Eva," Alejandro went on. "She sees how sad I am. I tell her everything and she is so kind, but she says I must tell my family. We talk and talk." He paused. "I will be honest with you now, Luke. Eva is beautiful. And I like her. It would not be so hard to do things with her. If there was no boy. If there was nothing else to do. But she always talks about her boyfriend. You. She loves you."

I stared at him.

"We came here. This very place. Yesterday. She told me she still loves you."

"She said that?" My mouth felt dry.

Alejandro nodded. "*Si*."

"About me?"

Alejandro grinned. "Please do not think again that I am trying to kiss you, but you are good to look at too. Like Eva. You and she are good together. No?"

My head was spinning? Could that be true? It had to be. I mean, why would Alejandro lie about it?

Then it struck me.

It was Eve who'd lied.

A dead weight settled somewhere in my chest. Of course Eve didn't love me. If she did, she wouldn't have dumped me. And *she'd* be talking to me, not Alejandro.

Jealousy began its familiar creep through my veins. Eve had been *here*. With *him*. Telling *him* how she felt. I stared out to sea. I couldn't make out where the water ended and the sky began.

"So you will talk with her?" Alejandro said, motioning me back to the car.

I shrugged. Whatever Eve had said to him, nothing changed what she'd said to me.

I was jealous.

I was immature.

She didn't want me.

Alejandro gesticulated wildy with his hands. "*Mierda*. Why not talk?" He groaned. "Is it a macho thing? She dumps me, I no talk to her?"

"No," I said, opening the passenger seat door and getting into the car. "There's just no point. She said she didn't want to go out with me any more."

"But she loves you." Alejandro slammed his door shut and turned on the engine.

I screwed up my face. "She can't love me *and* not want to go out with me. Not both at the same time. That doesn't make sense."

Alejandro took both hands off the wheel as he reversed screechingly onto the road.

"She is a girl." He sighed and switched on the car radio. "With girls anything makes sense."

We drove along for a while, listening to the music.

"You should try boys," Alejandro said after a few minutes. "Much easier. You wanna do it? Yes. No. Do it. Don't do it. Is easy." He glanced at me. "It's a joke, OK? I don't mean you. . ."

"I know." I smiled at him, then turned away. "Thanks, but I'm stuck on girls."

I looked out at the olive trees flashing past the car.

Stuck on Eve.

Stuck on Eve.

Stuck on Eve.

20

Through with love

I woke later than I realised the next morning. Ryan was lying spreadeagled on his bed – still fast asleep. I staggered into the bathroom for a shower, thinking about last night. There was what Alejandro had said about Eve still liking me – which I was sure was totally wrong. And there was what Ryan had said about Marco being upset because of what I'd done with Catalina – which I was equally certain was totally true.

The only part of last night I actually wanted to remember was how it had felt with Catalina. The way she'd looked at me. The way she'd pressed up against me. Her curvy bum in that strip of leather. How we'd kissed. . .

Several minutes later I switched off the shower and grabbed a towel. I wandered back into the bedroom. Ryan was now on his back, snoring gently, his fringe splayed over his face. Lucky git – he didn't have any shifts this morning. Unlike me. I glanced at the clock by Ry's bed. I froze. Ten-thirty. My pool shift had begun half an hour ago.

I looked frantically round the room for clothes. Everything was in heaps on the floor. I grabbed a pair of shorts from a couple of days ago and yanked them on. Then I found the least rancid-looking Bonita Boy T-shirt from the pile of clothes at the end of my bed. Pulling it over my head I raced out and charged along to the pool.

It was crowded, as usual. I slowed to a stroll as I reached it, peering through the hotel guests to see who else was working the shift. I saw Chloe folding up towels and went over.

"Where've you been?" she snapped. "I had to cover for you with Jonno. Told him you weren't feeling well."

"Thanks, Chlo," I said. I looked round the pool, suddenly realising I was starving. "Have you got any food?"

Chloe rolled her eyes. "God, Luke, you're like a little kid." She jerked her thumb towards the pool bar. "They've probably still got some croissants down there. They're only supposed to be for the hotel guests but I guess you could ask."

I looked across to the bar. Marco was standing beside it. One of his friends from last night was serving. I gulped. Why did I have to be on pool duty with them? "Would you get a croissant for me, Chlo?"

Chloe looked at me. Then over at the bar.

"You are such an idiot." She turned on her heel and marched over to the bar, reappearing half a minute later with a croissant wrapped in a little paper bag.

"Thanks." I stuffed it into my mouth.

Chloe shook her head at me. "You got over Eve pretty quickly," she said.

I stared at her, my mouth full.

"I mean, I thought you were crazy about her. But going after Cat like that. Well, like I said to Eve last night, it shows she was right to dump you."

My eyes widened. "You *told* her?" I said, spluttering croissant onto the pool paving.

"Hey, can I get a Coke, please?" One of the hotel guests was calling from a nearby sun lounger, her voice impatient.

Chloe rolled her eyes. "I haven't got six hands, you know."

She stalked off towards the bar.

I shoved the paper bag from the croissant into my pocket and followed her. Grabbed her arm. "What did you say to Eve? Jesus, Chloe, why did you tell her?"

Chloe stared at me. "Why does it matter? Eve would've heard this morning anyway. All the staff are talking about it."

My stomach clenched. "Are they?"

Chloe nodded. "Well, laughing about it."

"What?"

Chloe sighed impatiently. "Laughing at you for going after Cat. Laughing at Marco for putting up with her. Laughing at her for being such a nympho. Personally I think it's really unfair. Okay so Cat's got a rep for doing stuff with guys and shoving Marco's face in it. But if she was a bloke they'd be all admiring and impressed."

"You mean she's snogged people in front of Marco before?"

"Oh yeah. All the time apparently. New guy every few weeks." Chloe turned towards the bar again. "She totally gets off on making Marco's life a misery."

I watched her walk up to the bar and collect a Coke from the barman. It was the guy I'd noticed that first night in the Garito. The thickset bloke who looked like Eve's ex, Ben.

Along the bar from Chloe, Marco glanced up at me.

His face said it all.

He was hurt. He was humiliated. He hated me.

I spun round and walked back to the towels, my heart thumping.

Why would Catalina rather make Marco look stupid than carry on making out with me – which I'd thought . . . no, which I was sure – she'd been enjoying as much as I was?

I picked up a wet towel and put it inside the laundry trolley next to the metal towel rack.

Alejandro was right. With girls, anything made sense.

As I turned away from the rack, a man hunched over a bundle of papers on a nearby lounger asked me to fetch him a coffee. I looked round for Chloe. She had delivered her Coke and was busy with a couple of little kids on the other side of the pool. The only other person on duty was Marco, still sitting at the bar. *Crap.* I couldn't keep asking Chloe to get drinks for me. I was going to have to go to the bar myself.

I walked over. "*Café con leche,*" I said, not making eye contact with the barman.

I could feel Marco beside me. Part of me wanted to say something.

Er . . . Sorry you saw me snogging your girlfriend last night.

Yeah, right. That'll work.

How about, *Sorry I snogged your girlfriend. She turned me on so much I forgot you existed.*

I thought not.

The coffee cup slammed down in front of me. I glanced up. The barman's face was centimetres from my own, his eyes narrowed, his lips bared. His face really did look like Ben's now. How Ben had looked just before he beat me up. A finger of fear wriggled down my spine.

"*Mierda*." The barman grabbed my shirt, then unleashed a stream of Spanish at me. I didn't understand a word, but the meaning was clear.

His voice was low, snarling, full of venom.

Just like Ben's had been.

I was suddenly back there. The night Ben had beaten me up. It was happening again. The fists in my face. The kicks against my legs and arms. My heart started pounding. My hands shaking. Adrenalin coursing through me.

"So. You are shit," the barman finished.

He let go of my shirt and stood back, an expression of utter contempt on his face.

I picked up the coffee cup and turned away. Coffee splashed into the saucer. I'd freaked out before over Ben, but nothing like this. I tried to push away the panic rising in my throat. But it was too strong. Too powerful. I took a few steps. My legs were trembling. Coffee spilling everywhere.

What the hell was the matter with me? I couldn't breathe. My whole body was shaking. The coffee cup slipped out of my hands. Smashed to the floor.

In seconds Chloe was beside me. "Luke?"

I stared at her, panic filling me. Drowning me. *I can't breathe*. I gulped at the air. Trying to force it inside me. Gasping. Horrible gasping sounds. Heart racing. *Help me*.

Chloe's eyes widened. She put her arm round me. Pulled

me away from the pool. "Over here." She led me down towards the trees.

Still shaking. Still not breathing. Terrified.

Make it stop. Make it stop.

"Sit," Chloe ordered.

I slumped down beside one of the trees, hardly able to make out the ground in front of me. The blades of grass beneath my hands felt thick and rough. I pulled at the air. *Please let me breathe.* My hoarse gasps caught less and less of it.

Chloe grabbed the paper bag poking out of my pocket. She shook it out, then bunched it up round the edges. "Breathe out into this," she said. "Breathe out."

I took the bag. Tried to do what she said. Breathe out. *Omigod omigod.* Breathe out. All the air in my body was leaving it. Sucked out.

Help me.

"Now breathe in."

I breathed in. At last. A proper breath.

"Again," Chloe said, holding the bag against my mouth.

I took a few more breaths. Deeper ones. The shaking was subsiding, my heart rate slowing. I shivered and looked round at Chloe.

Hold me.

She put her arms round me and hugged me. We sat there

for a minute. As the tension slid out of my body a deep wave of misery welled up from the depths of my stomach. Chloe shifted back on her heels.

She frowned. "What was that about?"

"Ben," I said, shakily. "That guy. It was like when . . . when. . ." To my horror, tears bubbled up behind my eyes. I tried to swallow down the sobs, but my feelings still burst out of me.

"Oh, Chloe, I've screwed everything up," I choked. "I was such an idiot with Eve. And now. . ."

I stood up. My insides were a black hole. I was empty. Useless. I suddenly realised what I'd lost. Eve was everything. All the Catalinas in the world couldn't make up for losing her. I stumbled into the trees.

"Luke?" Chloe sounded anxious behind me.

"I'm fine. Just going for a walk."

"I'll say you're not well. Yeah?"

I nodded and strode off towards the beach without looking back.

I wandered along the shore. It was another beautiful, steamily hot day – clear blue sky, glittering sea. I reached the point where the sand turned into rocks. I leaned against the pale, washed-out stone and looked back along the beach. In the far distance a man and a little boy were playing football in the sand.

Otherwise I was alone.

I closed my eyes. Eve had loved me. And trusted me. And I had thrown all that back in her face by being jealous. A dull ache settled in my chest.

She'd been right to dump me.

I was a jerk.

I didn't deserve her.

I sank down onto the sand and sat, hunched over my knees, staring out to sea. It was so beautiful here. Naturally beautiful. Like Eve. Eve inside and out. *Oh God.* It was impossible to stay here another day. Impossible to be so close to her and to be so absolutely without her.

Half an hour later I'd made up my mind. I was going to go back to the hotel, march straight into the little office and email Mum that I wanted to come home early. Having a definite plan made me feel slightly better. I wiped my face and walked back along the beach.

My mobile rang as I reached the main lobby. It was Chloe. "Come up to my room," she said. "I need to talk to you."

"Why?" I said, not wanting to be deflected from my email.

Chloe was silent.

"Is something wrong? Chlo? Is it Eve?" My throat tightened. "Is it Mum?"

"Just come up." She rang off.

I shoved the phone back into my pocket. It rustled against a sheet of paper. The second scan of the baby that Mum had emailed. I'd forgotten all about it. My mouth was dry. Suppose there was something wrong with Mum's baby. With Mum. That was it. I broke into a run across the lobby, pounding up the stairs to the first floor.

21

Better together

By the time I'd reached Jonno's private flat, I'd convinced myself Mum must have had an accident. Lost the baby at the very least.

Chloe was waiting for me by the door. I followed her down the corridor and into her room. It was just like Eve's, only barer. A four-poster bed with fluttery pink curtains stood against the far wall while an ornate, white dressing table stretched the length of the window. It was all so completely not Chloe that I smiled, forgetting my anxiety for a second.

Then Chloe turned round. She looked nervous. My fears flooded back.

Chloe never looked nervous.

"What's happened to Mum?"

Chloe frowned. "Nothing. Mum's fine."

The flat's front door slammed. "That's not Jonno is it?"

Chloe shook her head. "He's in his office. For the next hour, we reckon."

"We?"

Voices sounded from the corridor.

"Okay, I'll do this if you promise me you'll talk to your dad." It was Eve.

I blinked. The door to Chloe's room swung open. Eve and Alejandro stood in the doorway. Eve was avoiding my eyes, looking stunning in her little shorts. I felt the familiar clench of desire I always felt when I saw her. I glanced at Alejandro. He grinned at me.

"Now, talk." He prodded Eve through the door. Chloe scampered over to him and they disappeared into the corridor, shutting the door behind them. I heard the key click in the lock.

I stalked past Eve and wrenched at the handle. The door wouldn't budge.

"I don't freakin' believe it. They've locked us in here." I thumped on the door. "Hey," I shouted. "Hey, let us out."

Silence.

"Don't you want to see me?" Eve said behind me.

I turned round.

She smiled nervously. "Are you okay? Chloe told me what happened earlier . . . what you said."

I stared at her.

"Alejandro and Chloe think we should talk to each other," she said.

What the hell was I supposed to do now? Bloody Chloe. How dare she interfere like this. I shoved my hands in my pocket. Felt the scan picture again. I pulled it out and looked at it. I still couldn't make out where the baby was. I walked over to the bed and sat down, staring at the paper.

It was easier than looking at Eve.

"Well, say something," she said.

I looked up at her and waved the picture. "D'you want to see this? It's Mum's baby again."

Eve looked mildly exasperated, but she came and sat down beside me. She peered at the grainy lines of the scan.

"Hey," she said. "This one's much clearer. Look. There's its head. It's lying curled up. See?" She pointed. "It's sucking its thumb."

I stared more closely at the picture, following the invisible tracing of Eve's fingers. And I saw it. The baby. Perfect and tiny. Sucking its thumb. It suddenly hit me. The baby was real. A real person.

I looked up at Eve, my eyes shining. "That's my little brother."

For a moment I forgot about everything else – it was just us again. The two of us, together and happy.

Eve moved her hand slightly and our little fingers

touched. I wanted her so badly. But it was different from how I'd wanted Cat. All the desire was there – the lust shooting through me. But there was something else too. Some scary feeling in the middle of my chest when I looked at her. She had so much power over me, power to hurt me. Part of me wanted to get up and run away.

But I couldn't take my eyes off her face.

And, anyway, they'd locked the door.

There was a long pause.

"Do you want to go out with Catalina?" Eve said.

"No," I said, honestly.

"But you fancy her?"

"Yes."

Eve recoiled a little. She picked up the scan and folded it. *Crap. Too honest, Luke.*

"But not like I do you," I added.

"So you fancied her that day in the store room too?"

"Sort of." I hesitated. "But nothing happened, honest. I didn't lie about that."

"Nothing happened *then,* you mean." Eve looked up at me. "When I heard about you and her last night I felt like my skin was all peeled open. I couldn't bear it."

"It was just a kiss," I mumbled uncomfortably. "It was stupid. Didn't mean anything."

Eve's pale eyes pierced through me. "Chloe said you had

your hands all over her. She said you were practically doing it on the dance floor."

Cheers, Chloe. Remind me to tell Ryan how you wet yourself once when you were ten.

I had no idea what to say. I shrugged.

"Feeling jealous is horrible," she said. "I realised last night what it's been like for you. I wanted to kill you. If you'd been here, if I'd seen you together, I might have tried. It was scary how awful it felt."

I nodded. "I know. But you never did anything to make me jealous. I was a moron. It was all in my head." I glanced at her. "Alejandro said you'd made up that stuff about liking him."

Eve blushed. "Actually, I did fancy him a bit. I mean, I wouldn't have done anything but he *is* incredibly good-looking. And he's so nice too."

I swallowed, waiting for the hard, dirty pull of jealousy to suck me down again. But it didn't come. And in that instant I realised – people were always going to fancy Eve. And she was bound to fancy some of them back. Maybe even be tempted by them. Just as I had been with Cat. But, like Ryan said, what was the big deal? Either Eve wanted to be with me – in which case I had nothing to worry about – or she didn't. In which case, all the worry in the world wouldn't save me.

I stared down at the folded-up scan. "I'm sorry about being jealous before," I said. "And I'm sorry about Cat."

And I'm sorry I blew it. So, so sorry.

"I'm sorry I dumped you," she said.

I shot a look at her.

"I mean, then you wouldn't have gone off with Catalina." Eve put her hand on my cheek. "Would you?"

The touch of her fingers rocketed straight to my groin. "Mmmn."

Eve's lips trembled.

S*hit.* "I mean no. No."

Eve drew her hand back.

I grabbed it.

How could I be so stupid?

"Eve. I wouldn't go off with anyone, ever. I swear. I don't want anyone else."

She got up and walked to the door. "I'm scared."

"Me too." I leaped up and followed her. "I'm scared too. Part of me wishes I didn't feel like I do. But I do. I can't help it."

Eve turned round and leaned against the door. She looked up at me. *God,* she was so incredibly beautiful. I put my hands on either side of her head, letting the door take my weight, then bent down so my face was right next to hers. We stood there, looking at each other.

"Please, Eve." My voice cracked. "I love you. I love you so much it—"

She was kissing me before I'd even finished speaking – this long, deep, sexy kiss that practically had me on my knees.

When I drew away, Eve's eyes were still shut, a blissed-out smile on her face. "I love you too," she whispered.

I moved towards her again. But her eyes snapped open.

"No," she said. "I'm fed up with being scared. You were right. Come on."

She turned and banged on the door.

I stared at the back of her head, bewildered. What was she talking about?

"Chlo! Alejandro!" she yelled. "Let us out. It's okay now. It's sorted."

I reached round her waist. "You mean it?" Happiness spread through me like fire. I kissed her neck. Sorted. She'd said it was sorted. *Yes.* I bit gently into her shoulder. *Mmmn*, she smelled fantastic.

Eve was still banging on the door. "Chloe. For God's sake."

Footsteps in the corridor. Then the sound of a key turning in the lock.

The door opened. I looked up, my arms still wrapped round Eve.

Chloe screwed up her nose. "I hope you haven't messed up my room," she said.

I made a face at her, then squeezed Eve closer.

"Let's go into your room and lock the door there," I said.

"No." Eve grabbed my hand. "Come *on*." She pulled me past Chloe and down the corridor.

Grumbling, I let her lead me out into the main part of the hotel. "Where are we going?"

Eve said nothing, just dragged me by the hand down the stairs.

I sighed loudly, but the truth was I didn't care where we were going.

She was holding my hand.

She wanted me back.

I'd have gone anywhere she said.

Hang on. She was holding my hand? She never touched me while we were in the hotel. As we reached the main lobby she was *still* holding my hand. I glanced at her, feeling nervous.

The last thing I wanted to do was pull it away, but what about Jonno?

We headed through the practically empty lobby towards the little office where I'd had to do my homework. I frowned. Then I realised where we were going.

Jonno's office was right next door.

Eve stopped in front of it and knocked – three loud raps.

She was still holding my hand.

22

Facing Jonno

"Come in." Jonno's voice was gruff. Surly. He did not sound in a good mood.

I stared at Eve. What the hell was she doing?

I moved my mouth but no words came out.

Eve pushed at the door. "Let me do the talking," she said.

About what?

I followed her into Jonno's office. It was a large, square room. Air-conditioned, I noticed immediately, unlike my broom cupboard next door. A leather sofa and chairs were at one end, near a door that opened out onto a patio at the side of the hotel.

Jonno himself was sitting behind a large desk in the corner. It was covered with files and papers and a PC and printer.

He glanced up at Eve. "What is it, Babycakes? I'm busy."

"I need to talk to you, Dad."

I suddenly realised why she wasn't letting go of my hand.

Oh.

Crap.

I looked back at Jonno. He'd clocked our hands too. He glared at me, his nostrils flaring.

I had a sudden image of Alejandro backed up against the wall outside the stage door, Jonno's fist round his throat. My heart started racing.

"Let go of her," Jonno barked.

Eve gripped my hand tighter. Her face was white. Determined.

"Luke and I are going out together," she said. "He's my boyfriend."

I could feel my palm spitting sweat into Eve's hand. Jonno's face hardened into an angry mask. Jaw clenched. Eyes staring. He stood up.

"No," he said. "He's not. You're too young to have a boyfriend."

"Dad, I'm sixtee—"

"Get out," he yelled at me.

I backed away. I guess it sounds pathetic, but most of me was wishing Eve would let go of my hand.

She didn't.

"If he goes, I go," she said.

Jonno stormed round from his desk and grabbed Eve by the shoulders. He looked so angry that for a fraction of a second I thought he was going to hit her. I lurched towards him, my fear transforming to rage.

Eve clutched my hand tighter, tugging me back.

Jonno ignored me. He lowered his head so it was closer to Eve's.

"Babycakes, you just don't understand boys." He jerked his head in my direction. "He doesn't care about you. Pilar caught him in the crèche with someone just the other day. He only wants—"

"Sex," Eve snapped. "I know. So you keep telling me. But guess what? The thing in the crèche was a . . . a misunderstanding. And we're not having sex. Luke's not even pushing me to have sex."

Jonno glanced at me, suspiciously. "What's wrong with him?"

My temper flared. "Nothing's wrong with me."

I could feel my face reddening. *Jesus.*

"Dad, listen to yourself. You have this one way you think all blokes behave. They don't all think about sex all the time, you know. Some of them want a relationship."

I looked at the carpet.

Jonno snorted.

"Luke's really sensitive. He listens to me. In fact, we talk more than anything else. He's really sweet – and nice."

God, she was making me sound like a total wimp.

"You're still too young," Jonno said.

"So when will I be old enough?" Eve let go of my hand at last. "I'm not a little girl any more. Why can't you see that?" She glanced at me. "Luke knows me better than you do. He made me realise. I've . . . I've acted all babyish around you for years because I was scared you wouldn't love me if I was grown up." Her mouth trembled. "But I was wrong, wasn't I Daddy? You'll let me grow up and still love me?"

A tear trickled down her face.

Jonno slid his arms round her and pulled her into a hug.

I took a couple of steps away from them. Funny. I didn't feel jealous at all.

"Of course I'll always love you," Jonno whispered, soothingly. He raised his head and glared at me over Eve's shoulder. "You're my princess. My number one girl."

He raked his fingers through his hair as Eve drew back, wiping her cheek.

She smiled up at her dad. "So you're okay with it? Me and Luke?"

Jonno's mouth curved into a smile.

It didn't reach his eyes.

"I'm not ecstatic but, like you say, you're growing up and so long as it doesn't go too far, I guess there's no harm in innocent friendship."

I frowned. No way did Jonno think it was innocent friendship. What was he playing at now?

Eve hugged him. "Thanks, Dad." She grinned at me.

"Now you guys better get out of here," Jonno said, walking back to his desk. He leaned against the edge of it, tapping one of his fat cigars against his palm. "I've got a lot of work to do."

Eve skipped to the door.

I walked after her, watching Jonno the whole way. I didn't quite trust him not to leap forward and shove his cigar up my nose or something.

His eyes followed my feet to the door, the cigar still tapping against his hand. Then he looked up.

"Luke?"

Now he gets my name right?

I stiffened. "Yes?"

Jonno looked past me to Eve. "Just give us two minutes, Babycakes. Man to man."

I turned to Eve.

Don't leave me here.

But she was smiling at her dad. "I'll wait outside," she said.

Boom. The door shut. I swivelled awkwardly. Jonno was still leaning against his desk. He put down the cigar and walked slowly towards me.

I gulped, trying to work out where I should try hitting him if he punched me. He was bigger and taller than me, but he did have a slight paunch. I clenched my fist, ready to drive it into his stomach.

Jonno loomed over me. His eyes narrowed.

"You little shit," he hissed. "You'd be flat on your back right now if I didn't think knocking your lights out would make my daughter even more convinced you're God's bloody gift."

I gritted my teeth as he clapped his hands down heavily on my shoulders.

"But let me tell you this," he went on. "If you hurt her, I promise I will kill you."

What a total idiot.

"I'm not going to hurt her." I shoved his hands off my shoulders. "Didn't you hear what she said?"

Jonno snorted. "Yeah. I heard, Mr Sensitive."

God. The man was a monster. In spite of being practically psychotic about keeping guys away from Eve, he was actually sneering at me for *not* managing to have sex with her.

"Is that it?" I snarled.

202

"No." Jonno gave me a withering look. "Whatever Eve thinks, I know exactly what's going on inside your filthy little head. And when you do, finally, get up the nerve to go for what we both know you're really after – know this – you're not getting it. Ever. Understand?"

Now I wanted to punch him.

I should have just walked out. But I was too angry.

I had to show him I wasn't some pathetic wimp. That he couldn't order me about. That whatever Eve and I did was up to us.

"Oh you don't need to worry about *that*," I said sarcastically. "I'm Mr Sensitive – remember? I'll let Eve decide when *that* happens."

And then I did it. I couldn't resist it.

I raised my eyebrows and smirked at him.

And it's going to happen soon, you bastard. Because she wants me. She really does. You should see the way she kisses me.

Jonno grabbed my T-shirt and bunched it under my neck.

Shit.

My whole body tensed. For a second I thought he was going to hit me after all. Then he let go of me, his jaw clenched.

"This isn't over." He breathed out heavily, then pushed me away.

I backed away to the door. Opened it. Slid outside.

Eve was waiting for me, her face creased in a huge grin.

As I saw her, I relaxed. After all, what could Jonno do?

I'd got Eve. He was beaten. *Stupid old bastard.*

I'd got Eve.

I grabbed her hand and we raced out of the hotel, past the screaming kids in the pool and along the beach – right along to the end.

We stayed there all day.

Bliss. Just me and Eve.

Heaven.

23

Beyond the sea

The last few days of the holiday were far and away the best. Everything was exactly how I'd hoped it would be before we set off. Lots of time for me and Eve to be together.

Not that we didn't mix with other people. We hung out with Ryan and Chloe and Alejandro and loads of the hotel staff. The first time Eve and I went to the Garito I was bricking it. But Ryan had worked his usual charm with Marco's mates. They weren't exactly pleased to see me. But at least the guy who looked like Ben didn't shout at me again.

Eve got a lot of attention. Now it was clear Jonno's rule about her had been broken and I was openly going out with her, half the blokes who worked at the hotel seemed to think they were in with a chance to steal her away when my back was turned.

I was furiously jealous.

Only joking.

I mean, I didn't much like them hitting on her, but it was only – what did Ryan call it? – harmless flirting. I even began to enjoy watching her fending them off, knowing she was waiting for me to come back.

We didn't see Marco and Cat for two nights. Then the next evening, while I was getting a beer, I spotted Marco on the other side of the room. He was chatting with Ryan, Chloe and Eve. I frowned, wondering if I should go over.

A small hand squeezed my arm. I turned.

Catalina. In her micro mini.

"Hi, *Rubio*," she said.

Some kind of invisible magnet pulled my eyes down to her skirt. *Oh, God.* I glanced over at Eve. She was laughing at something Ryan and Marco were saying. She didn't appear to have noticed Catalina.

I shook off Cat's hand and took a step away from her, back towards Eve. She grabbed my arm again.

"Hey." Her mouth twisted into a smile. "Don't you want having fun with me?"

I stared at her – at the mean glint in her eyes. "No," I said.

The music swirled all around us. Loud and fast and hard.

"*Por que?*" she said. "Why?"

"Several reasons." I pulled my arm free again. "Marco. Eve. Mostly me, actually."

Cat shrugged. "So what? Who care Marco? He always come back to me."

I shook my head. Turned away. And walked into Eve.

Our eyes met.

Catalina grabbed my arm for a third time. "Hey," she snapped at Eve. "I am here first."

The music pounded in my head. I kept my eyes fixed on Eve.

She stared back for a second, her expression unreadable, then shot an icy look at Catalina.

"Get your hands off my boyfriend."

There was a long pause. Catalina's eyes widened theatrically. She peeled her hand off my arm and held it in front of Eve's face, fingers spread.

"Is all yours," she hissed. She sashayed off into the crowd.

I didn't even think about watching her. I just carried on looking at Eve. "I wasn't going to. . ."

"I know," she said. "But still. . ."

I grinned and put my arms around her. Across the room Catalina ran her silky fingers across the back of Marco's neck. He turned and beamed at her. *Poor bastard.* I held Eve more tightly. People were pouring past us onto the dance floor as a new track pounded away. I leaned down and breathed her in.

She was beautiful. She was sexy. She was fun. She was sweet.

And she wanted me. No-one else.

There was no downside.

The last two days sped past. The last pool shift. The last waiting tables shift. The last evening.

I was waiting for Eve by the pool. It had gone eleven and she was supposed to have met me at ten-thirty. Even allowing for her notorious lateness, I was starting to get a little worried. Ryan and Chloe were off somewhere on the beach. I leaned impatiently back in my lounger. The underwater lights of the pool cast soft green shadows through the water.

I'd stationed myself at the end furthest away from the pool bar, which was still busy with hotel guests.

"*Hola*," Alejandro's voice behind me made me jump. I twisted and looked up. He was peering down at me from over the top of my lounger. "Hey. We must you know . . . how do you say . . . stop meeting like this."

I stuck my middle finger up at him.

He chuckled and came and sat on the next lounger. "You are waiting for Eva?"

I nodded, then checked the time. "Why aren't you playing? The band doesn't finish for half an hour."

Alejandro grinned. "I took the night off," he said. "Jonno said it was okay. He has been great with me. He said nothing to my dad. But he said, like Eva, that I must speak with him. So I did. Today. I told my dad. Told him everything. Being gay. Everything."

I stared at him. "How'd he take it?" I said.

Alejandro waggled his hand horizontally in the air. "So-so," he said. "No happy but at least he did no kill me." He stared at the pool, at the water lapping against the side. "I will be in the hotel for only a few more weeks. Then I will be free to tour. Get away from here." He looked up. "Hey." His voice was suddenly concerned. "*Mira*. Look. It's Eva. Something is wrong."

I shot up off the lounger.

Eve was running towards us out of the main lobby. Even in the dim glow of the terrace fairy lights I could see she was crying.

We reached each other on the grass between the pool and the terrace. She flung herself into my arms, now sobbing loudly.

"What is it?" I said, suddenly terrified. "What's happened?"

"It's my dad," Eve said. "He's ... oh God ... he's making me stay." She hugged me. "Oh, Luke, he's making me stay here."

What?

I held her away from me, trying to see her face.

"What d'you mean?" I said. "Making you stay in the hotel? He can't. For how long?"

"No." She wiped her eyes. "In Spain. In some school he's got lined up. I don't know for how long – he says until Christmas at least. He says now I've got my GCSEs it's a good time for me to try something new. And . . . oh Luke . . . I have to go *now*. Tonight."

"What?" It came out as a whisper. My stomach felt like it had fallen out through my shoes.

Eve's face crumpled again. "He says he can't trust me to behave myself in England. He's convinced you're going to try and shag me once we've been back five minutes. It doesn't matter what I say to him. He says he knows from something you said or how you looked at him or something. He's mad. He won't listen." She leaned against my shoulder and wept.

My heart sank, remembering how I'd smirked at Jonno in his office.

And it's going to happen soon, you bastard. Because she wants me. She really does. You should see the way she kisses me.

"What about your mother, Eva?" Alejandro stood beside me, his arms folded.

I nodded. He was right. Eve's mum wouldn't let this happen. She might be a bit pathetic where Jonno was con-

210

cerned, but surely she'd stand up to him for Eve's sake.

I held Eve away from me again. "Yeah, whatever your dad says, your mum's got . . . got rights, hasn't she?"

"It's not that simple." Eve's lips trembled. "I mean, my mum's got custody and all that, but my dad pays for everything. Mum hasn't had a modelling job for five years. Without his money she'd go to pieces."

"Can't your mum get a different job? I mean, there must be lots of things she could do."

"It's no good, Luke. He owns our house and everything in it. He owns our car. And he says if I don't do what he says he'll take them all back. And he'll take her to court and . . . oh, God, you know how threatening he can be." Eve started sobbing. "I told him I wouldn't go, but he just started going on about . . . about how Mum would be the one to suffer – like, how was she going to survive if he took all his money away. And . . . and I called Mum and she's upset but . . . but Luke, she's frightened of him. So she's saying it's just a few months, like that's hardly any time at all." She wiped her eyes. "I can't bear it. It'll be *ages* before I see you again."

Fury surged through me. "I'm going to stop him." I stormed towards the lobby door.

"How?" Alejandro grabbed my shoulder. "Hey. Luke. Stop. You will make everything worse for Eva."

"Then I'll stay too." I turned back to Eve and pulled her towards me. "He can't do all this, just to keep us apart."

"He can." Eve's voice was shaky. "He says we'll both lose interest once we're apart."

"*I* won't." My mind raced, trying to think of a way I could stay in Mallorca with her. Or come back and find her. "He must have said something about where you're going?"

"No." Eve looked up at me. "He won't tell me where it is. He doesn't want you to know."

Alejandro whistled. "He must be really angry at you," he said.

I hugged Eve tighter. This couldn't be happening.

Over Eve's shoulder I could see Ryan and Chloe walking up past the pool. Alejandro went over to them. I could hear him talking quietly, explaining everything. Ryan swore. Chloe gasped. I watched her hand fly up to her mouth. Then they both looked over at me and Eve.

I looked away, kissing Eve's hair. It didn't feel real. Surely, it wasn't real.

"Come in now, Eve." Jonno's voice boomed out from the main lobby doorway. He was standing with his legs apart, chewing on his cigar. I itched to walk over and ram it down his throat.

Eve disentangled herself from me.

212

"I have to say goodbye to everyone," she sniffed.

I caught her hand. "Now?" I said. "Right now?"

"Eve's leaving immediately," Jonno said. "Best to avoid long goodbyes, I always think. So easy to get carried away with them."

He glared at me.

Eve let go of my hand and walked down to the others. I watched her hug each of them in turn. I could see Chloe was crying.

I was numb. Surely I would wake up in a minute and this would be a dream.

Jonno clapped his hand on my shoulder. "Hope you enjoy next term, Mr Sensitive." He took a big puff on his cigar.

"You *bastard*," I said. "You can't do this."

Jonno grinned. "Watch me."

Eve came back. She ignored her dad and took my hand. "We're saying goodbye in private," she said, tugging me away.

"You've got two minutes," Jonno called out.

Clutching each other's hands, we stumbled past the pool, past the others. Through the trees. Onto the beach.

We stood on the sand, the warm breeze salty in our faces. Dazed, I looked round. Only a few other people strolling about. You couldn't even hear the Garito from here.

Eve hugged me. "Hold me," she said.

I held her, my head starting to clear. "Let's run away," I said. "We can go right down the beach, onto the rocks. Climb up. Walk into Cala del Toro. Hide."

Eve shook her head. "We wouldn't get anywhere in two minutes. Anyway, we don't have any money and my dad would find us." She paused. "I'm doing what he says so he won't hurt you, Luke."

"I can look after mys—"

"Sssh." Eve tilted her face up to me. Her eyes were red and puffy and her skin was marked with tear tracks. "Face it, Luke. He's won. For now, he's won."

I stared at her, letting what she said sink in, accepting what had to happen now. I smiled, as an old thought reoccurred to me.

"What?" she said.

"You're so beautiful," I said. "Even when you've been crying. You're more beautiful than anyone."

I leaned down and kissed her. I put everything I had into that kiss. Everything I felt for her. All my desire. All my heart.

"Don't forget me," I said.

"EVE!" Jonno's voice bellowed out from the hotel.

Man, was he standing there with a stopwatch or something?

I raised my eyes.

214

Eve smiled. "Don't come up to the hotel with me." Her voice faltered. "I want to remember last seeing you here, like this."

Something cracked in my chest. "We'll see each other soon, yeah?"

Eve nodded. Her eyes were desperate. "Wait for me."

"EVE!"

"I have to go," she said. She stood for a moment, staring at me.

Then she reached up and kissed me one last time.

"I love you," she said.

And she turned and ran away into the trees.

Ryan found me sitting on the sand ten minutes later. He took me down to the Garito. We sat on the step, listening to the music.

After a while, Chloe and Alejandro turned up with a bottle of tequila. We sat around drinking for hours.

At first, I thought the booze was helping. But then I was sick on the beach, walking back to the room – which, of course, felt totally rubbish.

Then it was morning. We had to leave before ten a.m. Jonno was still out, presumably wherever he had taken Eve. He had left instructions for one of the hotel clerks – an old guy who spoke very little English – to drive us to the airport.

I hardly said anything on the way home. I tried to text and call Eve several times, but her phone seemed to be permanently switched off.

Mum met us at the airport. I could see her looking round for Eve. Then Chloe explained what had happened.

Mum looked good. Really happy. And all fat round the middle. I told her I was pleased she was having a baby, and this time I meant it. She hugged me, but she didn't say anything about Eve until we got home and we were on our own.

Then she listened sympathetically as I raged about how unreasonable Jonno had been.

"But four months isn't *such* a long time, Luke."

I glanced at her. What was she talking about?

Mum smiled. "I mean, I know it feels bad right now, but Eve'll be back before you know it. And, you know, you're both still pretty young to be getting so serious about each other."

She just didn't get it.

I got a call from Jonno the day after we got home.

"I wanted to let you know Eve's settling in nicely."

"Where?" I said.

Jonno snorted. "Not telling you, sunshine. And don't bother asking Eve's mum. I've told her not to say anything, especially to you. Anyway, I'm calling to say you can stop phoning. They don't allow the girls to have mobiles where she is now."

"Sounds like a prison."

"Needs to be, mate," Jonno chuckled. "Keep little shits like you out."

"Why are you doing this?" I said, my temper rising. "Why is me being with Eve such a big deal? Such a big threat?"

Jonno laughed. I could hear him rolling his cigar around in his mouth. "You'll work it out as you get older," he said. "All other guys are a threat when it comes to girls like Eve."

He hung up.

I stared at the phone. Then, slowly, I smiled.

Okay, Jonno, I thought. You win for now.

I'll accept it. I'll get on with my life. Go back to school.

But you can't keep Eve locked up forever.

And when she's free, I'll still be waiting for her.

And there won't be anything you can do about it.

Turn over for a taste

of the next book

in the series,

The One and Only!

1
Missing Eve

Nothing hurt like missing Eve.

My girlfriend had been gone two months and I still thought about her every day.

Eve's dad had shut her up in some convent school in Spain. He worked out there, running a hotel where we'd spent part of the summer holidays. He'd said she'd have to stay in the school for a term – no boys, no phones, no way of contacting the outside world. He did it because of me.

Because of us.

I wasn't supposed to know it was a convent school – with bars on the windows like a prison and a starchy brown uniform – but Eve's mum had told me.

It had taken me two weeks of going round every day to get any information out of her. Even then, she wouldn't tell me the things I really wanted to know.

Like, where *exactly* was Eve's school?

Had Eve said anything about me?

When was she coming home?

I think Eve's mum was scared I'd get on a plane and go out to Spain and rescue her. Believe me, I fantasised about doing just that all the time. But I had no idea where she was. And no money to get there, even if I did.

Of course what Eve's mum was most afraid of was what Eve's dad would do if he found out she'd told me anything.

Eve's dad. Jonno. A total bastard. The person I hated most in the whole world.

It was Bonfire Night. The fifth of November. I was going out later with my best mate, Ryan, and some other friends. There was just time for a quick visit to Eve's mum's house to see if there was any news.

I trudged resentfully up the path. I didn't expect things to be any different than they had been on my last visit, about ten days ago.

But they were.

Eve's mum had obviously been crying. Her eyes were all red and puffy when she opened the door. 'Hello, Luke.'

I shuffled awkwardly on the doorstep. I liked Eve's mum. For a start, she looked a lot like Eve. The same long blonde hair and heart-shaped face. And she was always nice to me. But I wished she wouldn't get so emotional about everything.

'Er . . . you all right, Mrs Ripley?'

'No. Not really.'

My chest tightened. 'Is it Eve? What's happened? What's the matter?'

'Her dad's saying she's got to stay out there for a *year*.' Her voice trembled. 'A whole year.'

'He can't!' I stared at her. 'It's only supposed to be until Christmas. That's what you agreed. You can't let him *do* this.'

Eve's mum twisted her hands together. 'How can I stop him? He's got all the money. And he is her father.'

For goodness sake.

Privately, I thought Eve's mum was more than a bit pathetic when it came to Jonno. OK, so he was big and loud and aggressive – and he owned her house and everything in it. But still – she could have moved out. Got a job. Supported herself and Eve. Even if it meant being a bit poorer.

'He's probably just trying to frighten you,' I said. 'Have you talked to Eve about it?'

I knew Eve and her mum spoke once a week. Eve's mum was too scared of Jonno to risk letting me talk to Eve myself. And she didn't say much about their conversations, but at least I knew Eve was still alive . . . still thinking about me.

'Eve thinks staying for the year's a good idea.'

'What?' A cold line of fear snaked its way down my spine.

'She said that now she's settled in it makes sense to finish out the year. That if she stays she'll be able focus properly on her art studies.'

I frowned. I couldn't believe Eve really thought this. Jonno had probably been visiting that day . . . listening to her conversation. Still.

'Did she say anything about . . . about . . . ?'

Eve's mum smiled sadly at me. 'About you?' She hesitated. 'Actually she did.'

'Well?' I dug my hands deep into my pockets, hands clenched into fists.

Eve's mum sighed. 'She said the two of you should forget about each other.'

What? 'I don't believe you.'

'I'm not saying she meant it, Luke,' Eve's mum sniffed. 'She might have been saying it because she knew it was what her dad'd want to hear. But it's what she said. That it was stupid you both waiting about for a whole year. That you should move on.'

I nodded, thinking it through. I was sure Eve was just trying to convince her dad she was over me. Well, I was *almost* sure. My stomach twisted. Maybe what she'd said was what she really thought. It was unbearable not being able to talk to her myself.

I refused Eve's mum's offer of a drink and wandered off to the park, where I was meeting Ryan and the others. This nagging feeling that Eve had never made that much effort to stand up for herself against her dad had been worming through me for weeks. Now it forced its way to the front of my mind.

How can you be happy to stay in Spain for a whole year, Eve? If it was me, nothing would stop me getting back here to you. Nothing. Don't you want me any more? You didn't even call me on my sixteenth birthday. That was September, Eve. Now it's November. Where are *you?*

I walked through the trees at the entrance to the park. The wind was ice cold. Fierce. People all around me were tugging at their jackets to keep themselves warm.

Surely there's some way you could get in touch with me, Eve? Even if the school doesn't allow mobiles, it certainly has phones. And there must be a networked computer somewhere. Anyway, how hard could it be to borrow a stamp and get one of the other girls at the school to take a letter to a postbox for you?

I could see the top of the massive bonfire at the other end of the park. It glowed orange above the silhouettes of all the people standing, staring at the flames.

Have you met someone in Spain?

No. That couldn't be it. Jonno would hardly separate her from me and let her mix with other guys. I walked past the small pond where Eve and I had met up all through February half-term, when she was still going out with Ben.

So what then? Is it that you just don't feel the same any more?

The ground was littered with twigs and leaves from the trees above my head. I crunched across them, trying to reassure myself.

I'm not going to jump to conclusions. OK? It was like your mum said. You were saying what Jonno wanted to hear. Weren't you, Eve?

I had jumped to conclusions in the summer – over this Spanish guy. Eve had been in his room one night. She'd said nothing had happened but I hadn't believed her. Then it turned out he was gay and miserable about not being 'out' with his family and they had just been talking after all. Eve dumped me for not trusting her. The next few days until I got her back were hell.

I wasn't going to make that mistake again. And yet . . . it was hard to feel OK without any reassurance.

I could hear, as well as see, the big bonfire now. Hissing and spitting and crackling. Little kids were running about with sparklers, writing their names in the air. There was a square fence made of metal barriers set several metres away from the fire, surrounding it. People were pressed up against the metal bars, staring at the flames in the centre.

I stared too, admiring the way the fire licked and leaped, always moving, eating at the logs beneath it, twisting up into the sky.

I couldn't see Ryan or any of our friends, so I pushed my way through the crowd to get closer to the barrier. The heat from the fire was strong on my face, even at this distance. And then I felt a different heat. The sensation that someone was staring at me. I looked round. A girl I hadn't noticed before was standing next to me. As I met her eyes, she smiled.

She was pretty – with a small, round face and a dimple in her chin. And she had amazing hair – great waves of red curls that tumbled right the way down her jacket. The flames from the bonfire were lighting the curls, creating a golden halo effect around her head as if the hair itself was on fire.

'Hi,' she said.

I frowned. Did I know her? She *looked* familiar. Yes, I was sure I'd seen her before. But not at school. Somewhere else. With someone else I knew well.

'Haven't I met you before?' I said.

The girl's smile deepened, revealing two more dimples in her cheeks. 'That has to be the cheesiest line ever,' she said.

'It's not a line,' I said, feeling myself blushing. 'I wasn't . . . I didn't . . . I mean, I really thought I'd seen you somewhere.'

I turned awkwardly back to the fire.

God, Eve. See how crap I am without you?

'Oh.' I sensed the girl was still looking at me.

I stared at the fire, wanting to walk away, but feeling it would look rude.

'I'm sorry,' the girl said. She leaned forwards on the barrier, next to me.

I glanced down at her. She grinned.

'Luke! Hey, Luke, man.' Ryan raced over. 'Where've you been? Come on, this is rubbish. We're going down the Burger Bar.'

He punched me on the shoulder. Then he turned towards the girl. 'So who've you been chat— OH MY GOD. HAYLEY.'

'Ryan.' The girl's eyes were wide. The hiss of the fire and the low murmur of people chatting filled the silence.

Then Ryan stepped forward. With characteristic swagger he wrapped his arms around the girl and hugged her.

'Hey, where've you been, Hayley?' he said, twisting round to wink at me over the girl's shoulder. 'You just dropped off the face of the earth.'

The girl pulled away from him, making an obvious effort

not to smile. 'Actually *you're* the one who dropped off the face of the earth. After that party in February.'

'Oh, right.' Ryan looked sheepish. 'Sorry.' He gave her what I knew was his most charming grin. 'I must have been mad,' he said.

Hayley rolled her eyes. 'Yeah, right. I heard you started going out with some girl – Chloe somebody?'

It all fell into place.

'You were at our party,' I said. '*That's* where I remember seeing you.'

Leaving with Ryan and him snogging your face off at the end of our road.

Ryan and Hayley both turned to me.

'D'you remember Luke from then?' Ryan said. 'Chloe's his sister.'

Hayley stared at me.

'Hey, d'you wanna come with us down the Burger Bar?' Ryan said.

I watched Hayley. I really didn't care whether she came or not.

You see, Eve? I only care about you.

Hayley's face fell. 'I can't. I'm with my parents and my sister. We're going out for dinner at this really expensive restaurant. It's a great place, but . . .' She tailed off.

Ryan shrugged. 'No problem.'

Hayley hesitated. 'Maybe another time though.' She glanced at me, then back to Ryan. 'You know? Let me know if there's a good party on or whatever, yeah? Um . . . have you still got my number?'

Ryan grinned at her. 'Here.' He handed her his mobile. 'Put it in my phone. Next time I hear of a "good party" I'll call you.'

Hayley blushed as she punched in her number. She said goodbye quickly and scampered away.

As we wandered over to where our friends were standing, Ryan started writing a text. I peered over his shoulder. He was calling up Hayley's number.

'What are you doing?' I said. 'You can't call her straight away. In fact, you can't call her at all. What about Chloe?'

Ryan grinned at me. 'I'm just forwarding her number to you, you idiot. That's why she gave it to me.'

I stared at him. '*What?*'

'Lu- uke, man.' Ryan rolled his eyes. 'Didn't you see the way she looked at you? You should ask her out. One date's not going to hurt anyone.'

As he strolled away from me, my mobile beeped. I checked the text. There was Hayley's number next to a message from Ryan.

TLKS A LOT BUT FIT BDY. CALL HER.

Acknowledgements

With thanks to Moira Young, Gaby Halberstam, Melanie Edge, Julie Mackenzie, Sharon Flockhart and Caitlin McCarthy

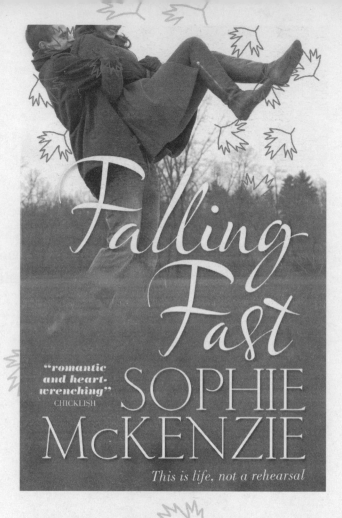

Falling Fast

"romantic and heart-wrenching"
CHICKLISH

SOPHIE McKENZIE

This is life, not a rehearsal

When River auditions for a part in an inter-school performance of Romeo and Juliet, she finds herself smitten by Flynn, the boy playing Romeo. River believes in romantic love, and she can't wait to experience it. But Flynn comes from a damaged family - is he even capable of giving River what she wants? The path of true love never did run smooth...

ISBN 978-0-85707-099-9 £6.99

"*romantic and heart-wrenching*"
CHICKLISH
on Falling Fast

Burning Bright

SOPHIE McKENZIE

Should love really be this intense?

Four months have passed and River and Flynn's
romance is still going strong. River thinks Flynn has
his anger under control, but when she discovers he
has been getting into fights and is facing a terrible
accusation at school, she starts to question both
Flynn's honesty - and the intensity of their passion.
Things come to a head at a family get together
when River sees Flynn fly into one unprovoked
rage too many. The consequences for both of them
are devastating and threaten to tear them apart
forever.

ISBN 978-0-85707-101-9 £6.99

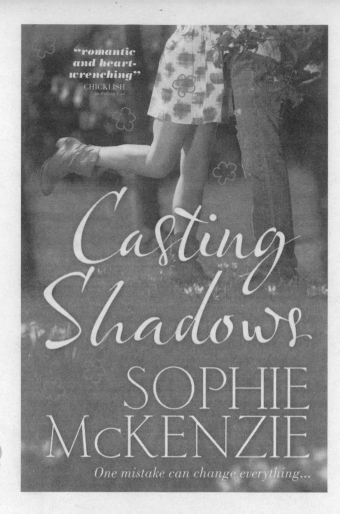

"romantic and heart-wrenching"
CHICKLISH
on Falling Fast

Casting Shadows

SOPHIE McKENZIE

One mistake can change everything...

Flynn is making every effort to stay in control of
his hot temper, while River feels more content than
she's ever been. Together the two of them make big
plans for the future, but powerful secrets lurk in
the shadows, ready to threaten their happiness.

ISBN 978-0-85707-103-3 £6.99